Mega Dungeon Maker

D100 Dungeon Chambers

Severed Books

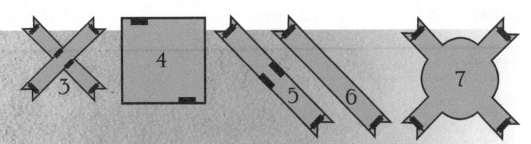

This book is a larger adaptation of the Dungeon Dealer card decks. You will literally never draw the same dungeon twice using this book. Even with a 52 card deck, there are so many combinations that if you are holding a well-shuffled deck, you are probably holding a combination of cards that have never existed in that order before. Search the "52 factorial" online and see what we mean.

This book has 120 chambers ("cards"), more than twice as many as a 52 card deck.

Each map section is numbered 1-100 with black numbers. Roll 2D10 to generate a random 1-100 number and draw the dungeon chamber you land on. You can turn the book in any direction to accommodate your map or roll 1D4 to orient the section north, east, south, or west using the red numbers. Use the hallway sections in the margins of the pages to draw hallways when you need them, either rolling a D20 or choosing the best one for your growing map.

Roll 1D20 to generate boss chambers.

Never draw over what you have already drawn. Just draw as much of the new chamber as you can without overlapping.Never feel pigeonholed. You can add doors and other elements whenever you like. Traps and some doors are triggered by corresponding color (red) circular floor plates on the map.

Lastly, have fun! This book is meant to surprise even the most seasonsed Game Master.

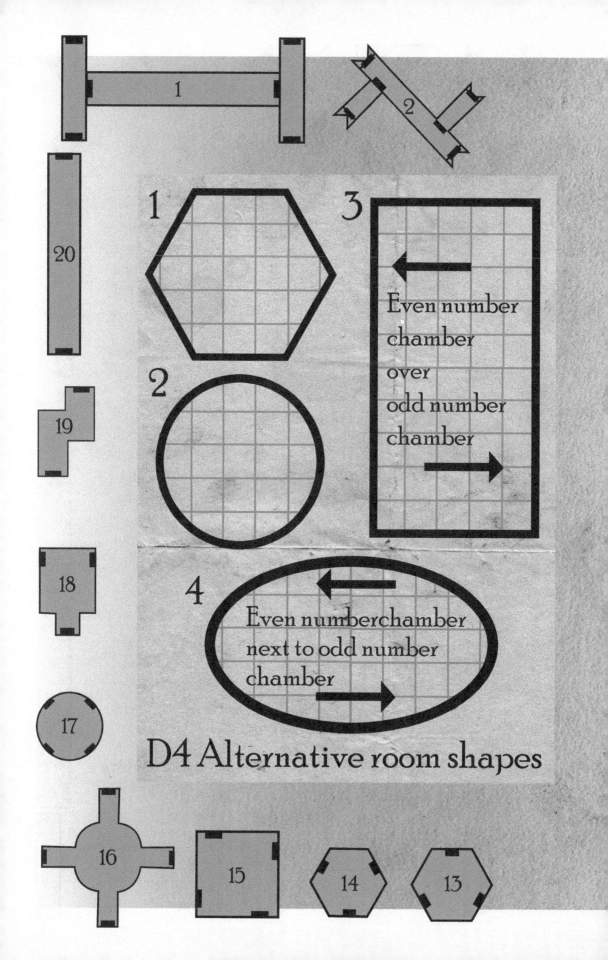

1

2

1

2

3

Even number chamber over odd number chamber

4

Even numberchamber next to odd number chamber

D4 Alternative room shapes

20

19

18

17

16

15

14

13

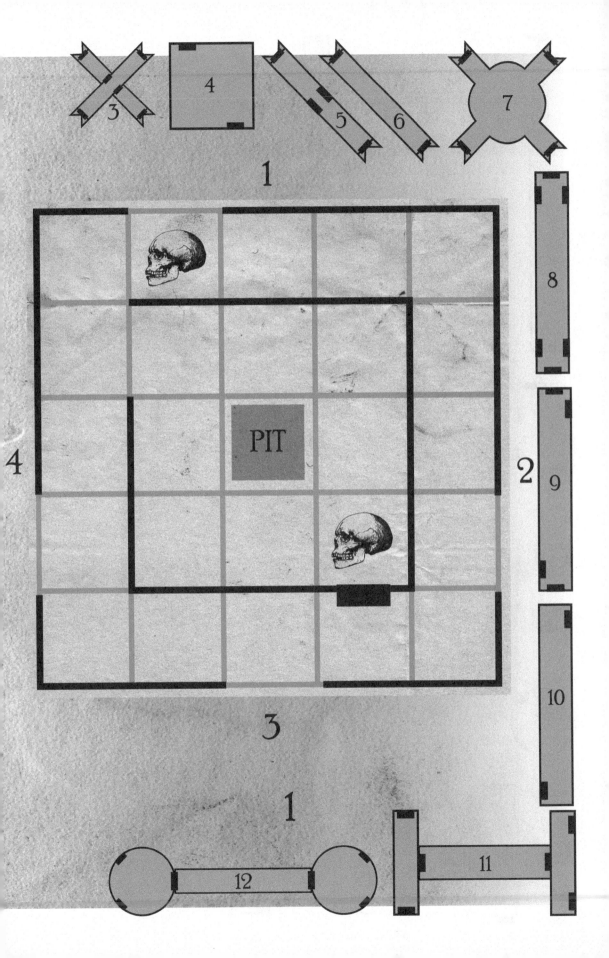

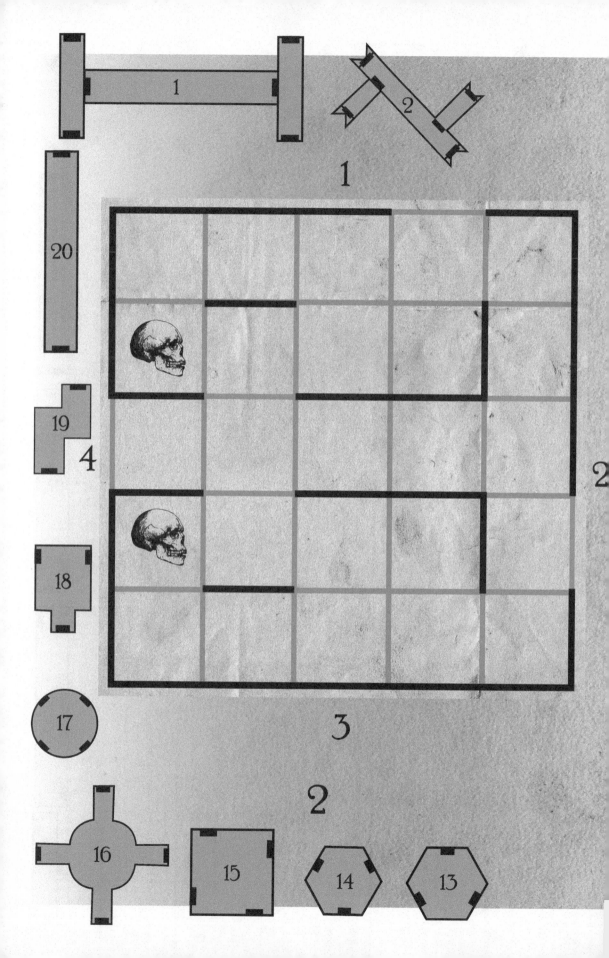

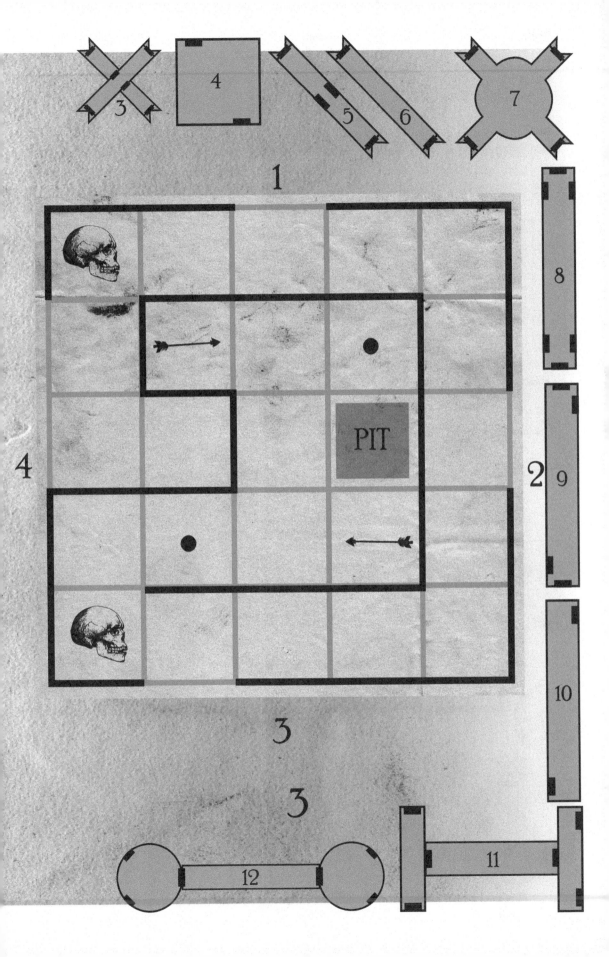

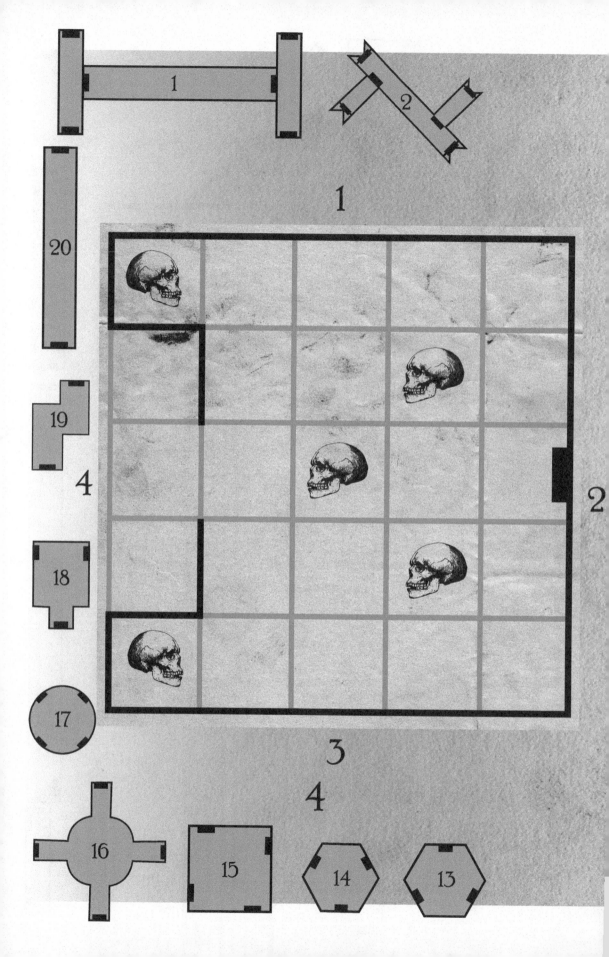

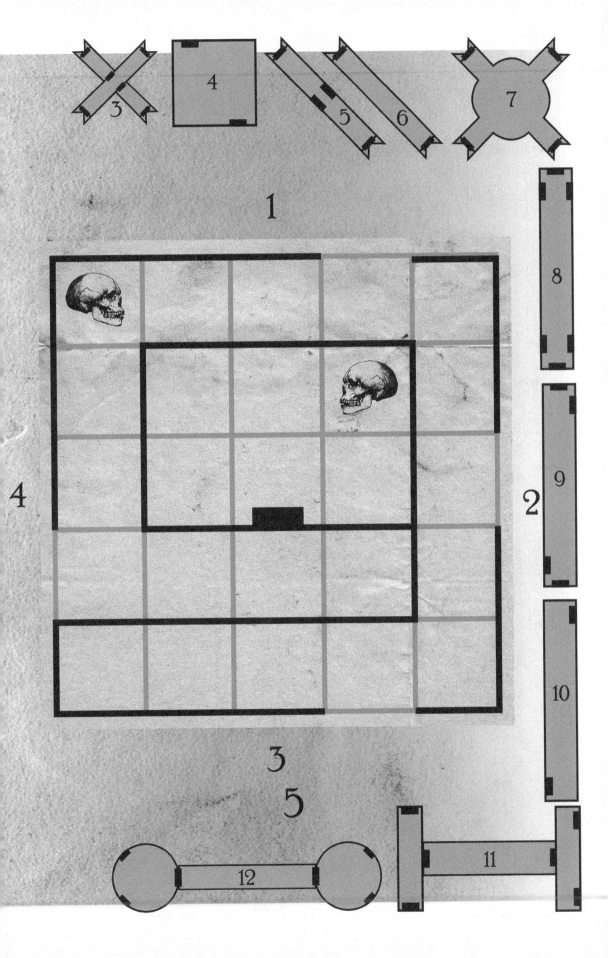

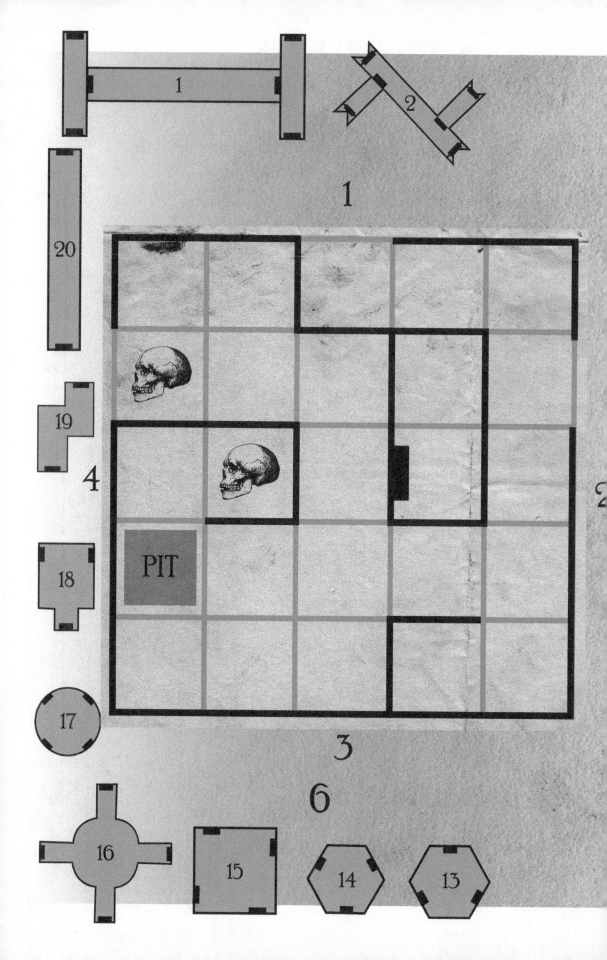

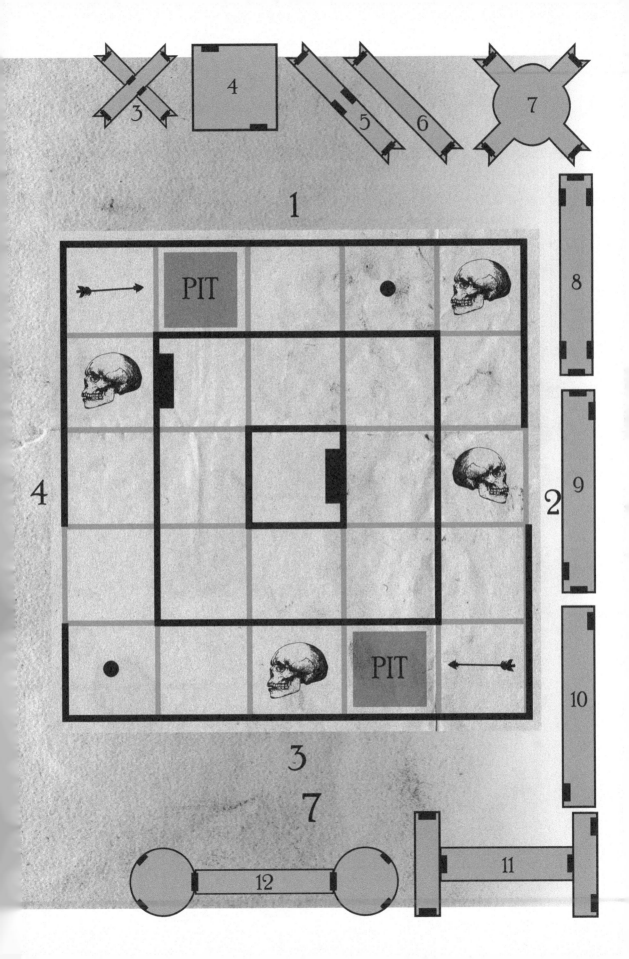

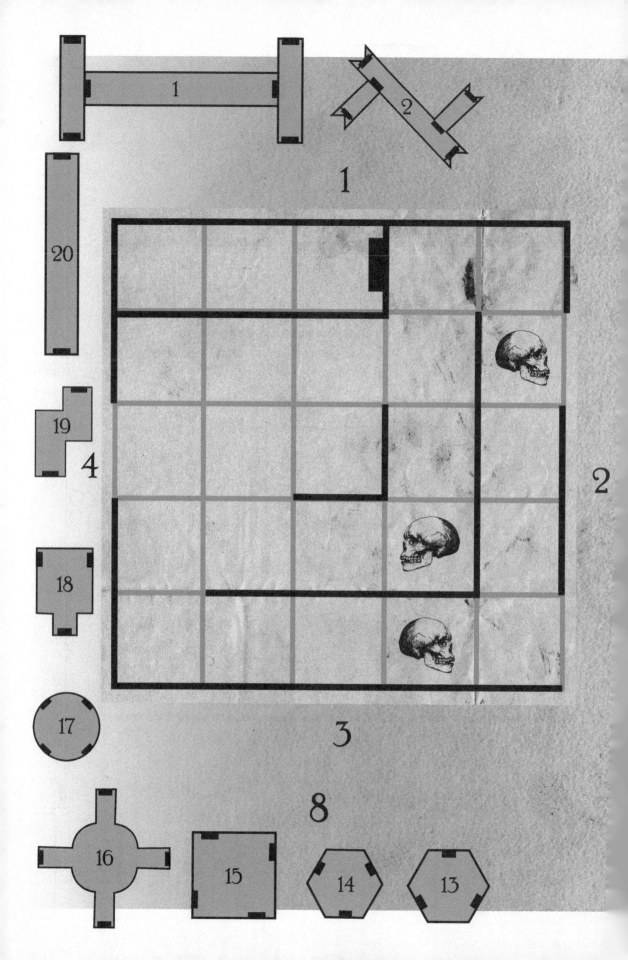

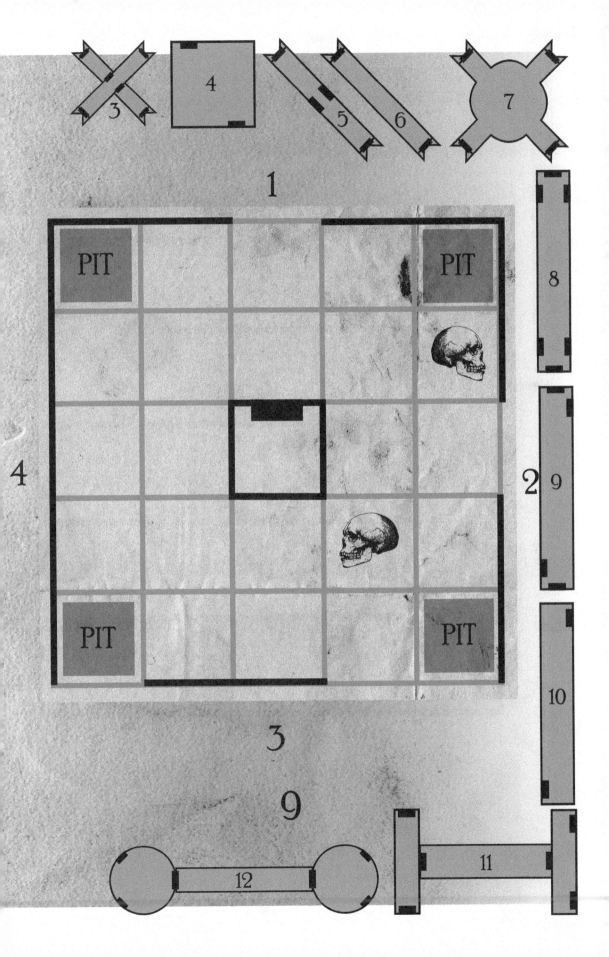

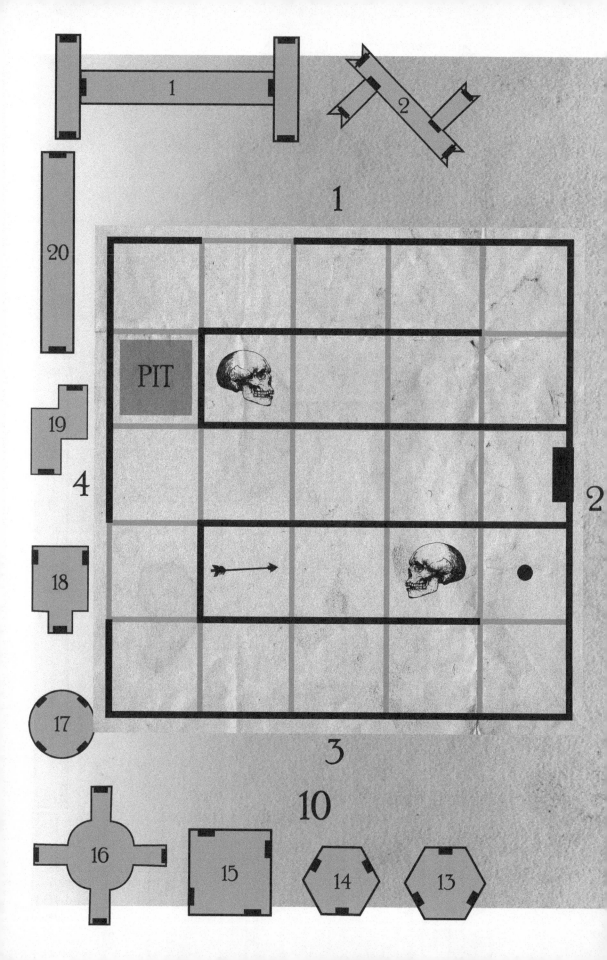

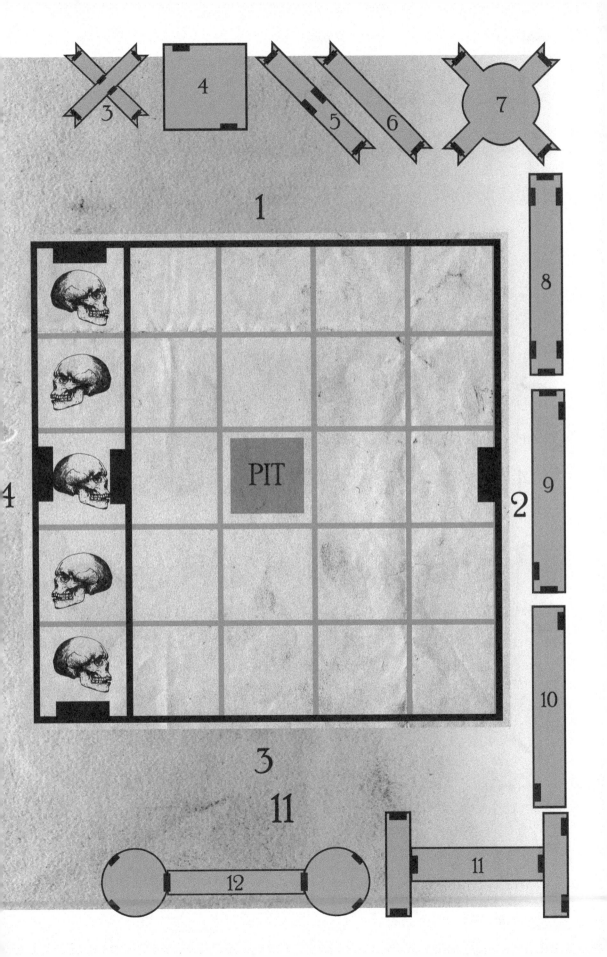

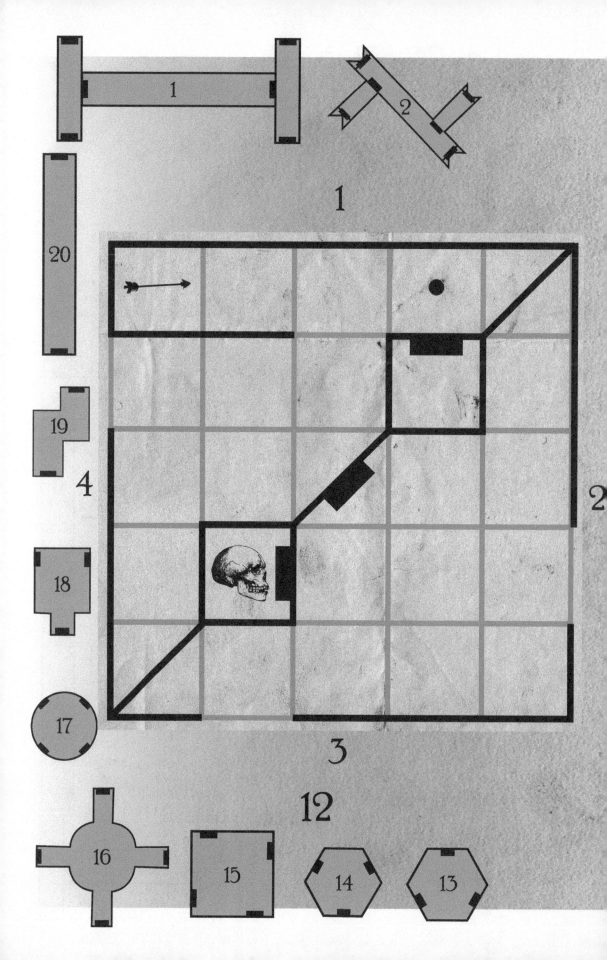

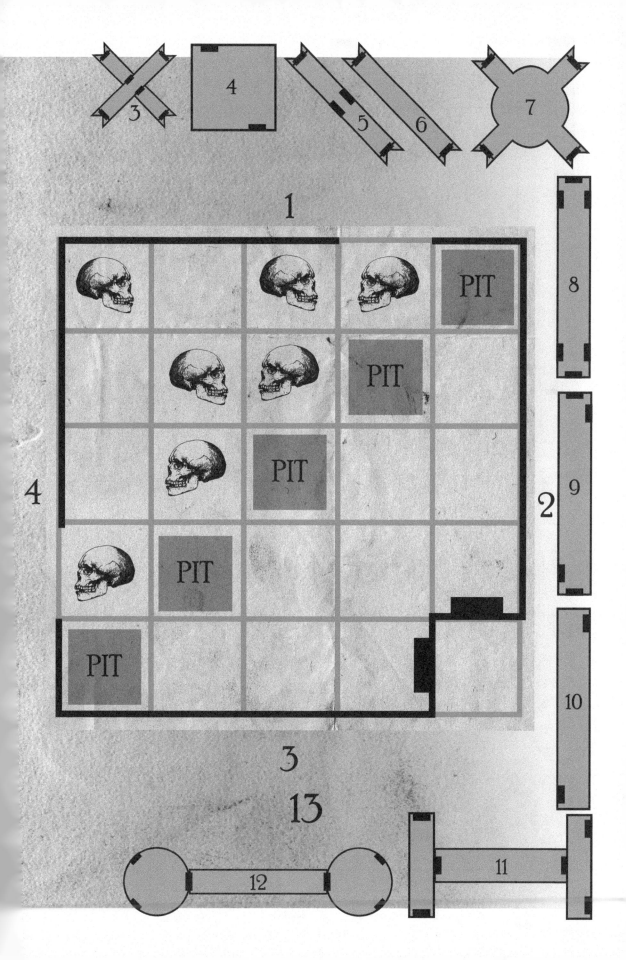

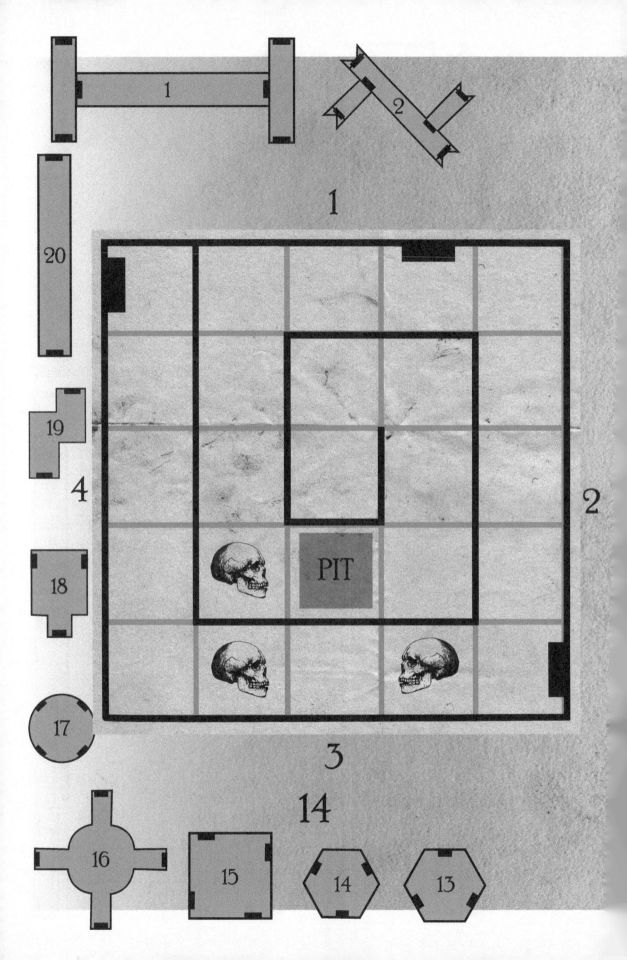

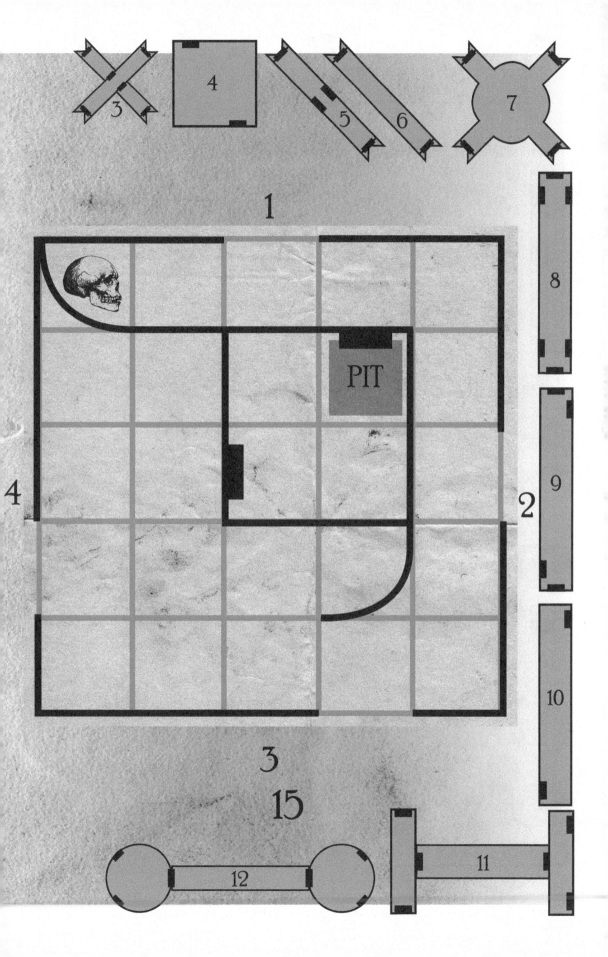

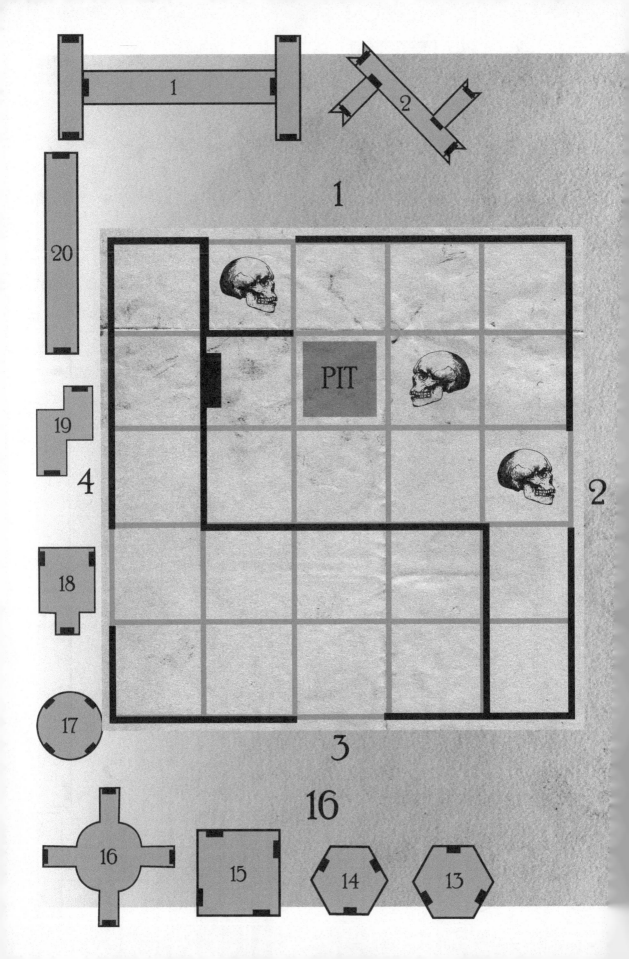

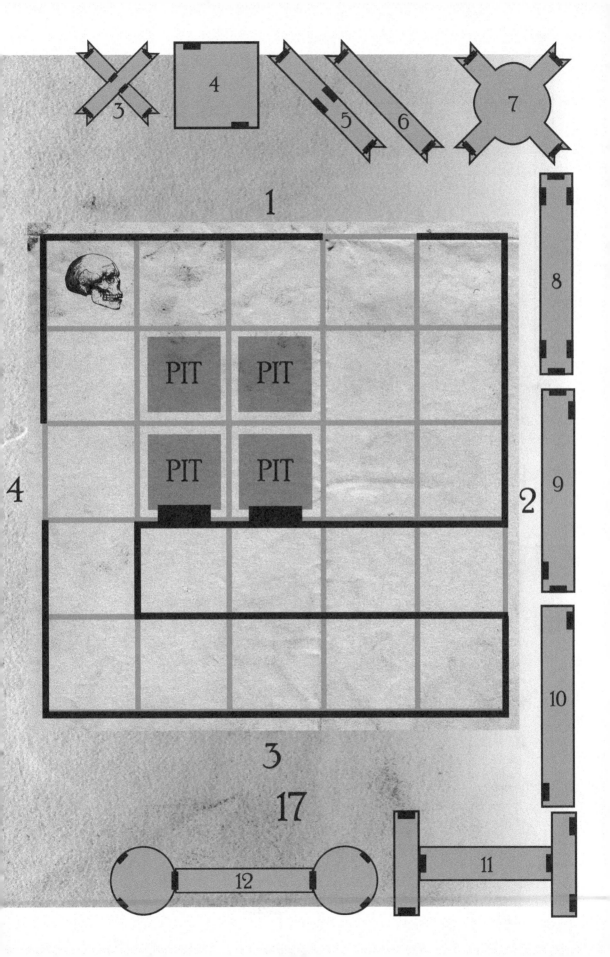

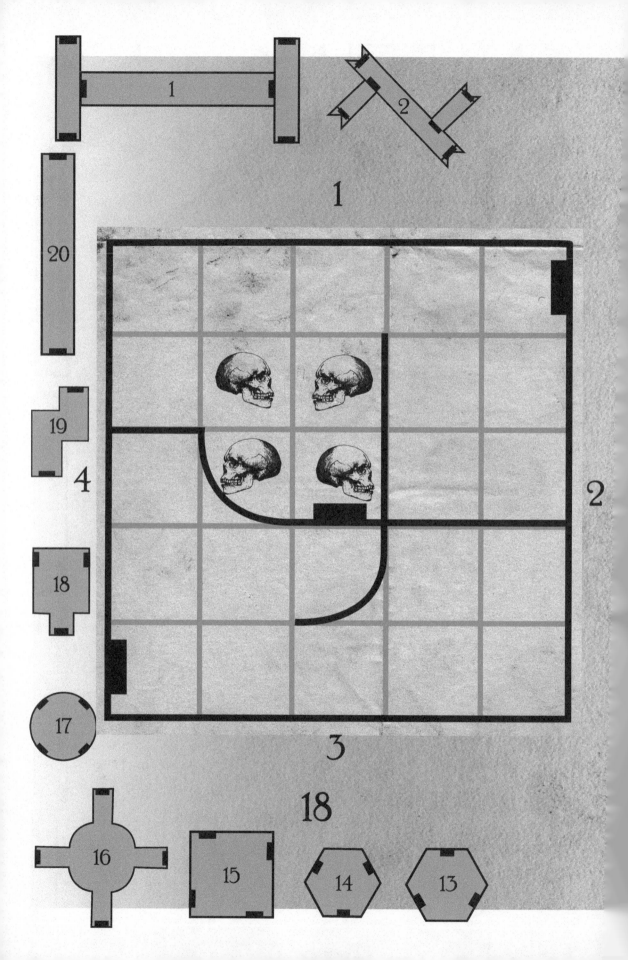

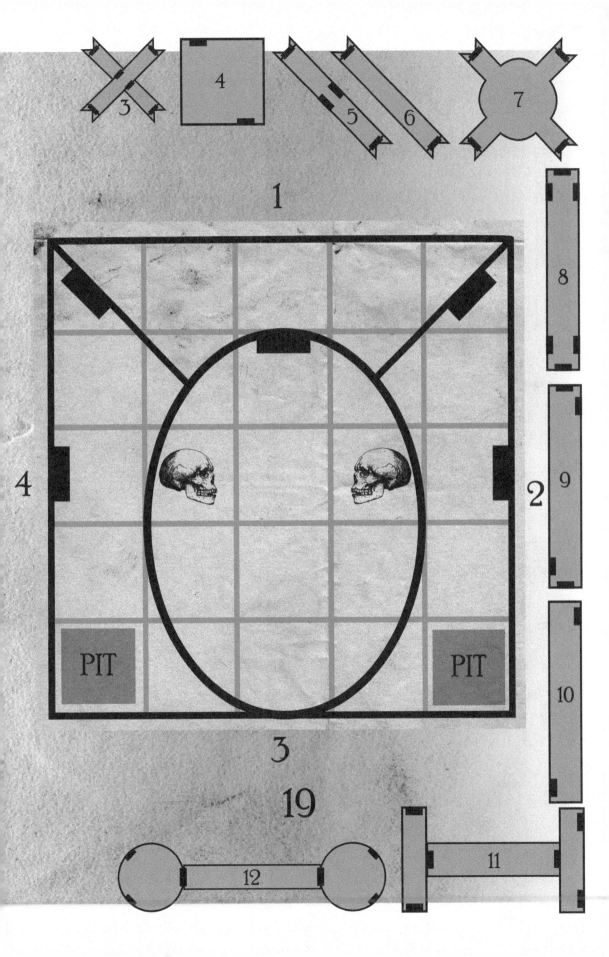

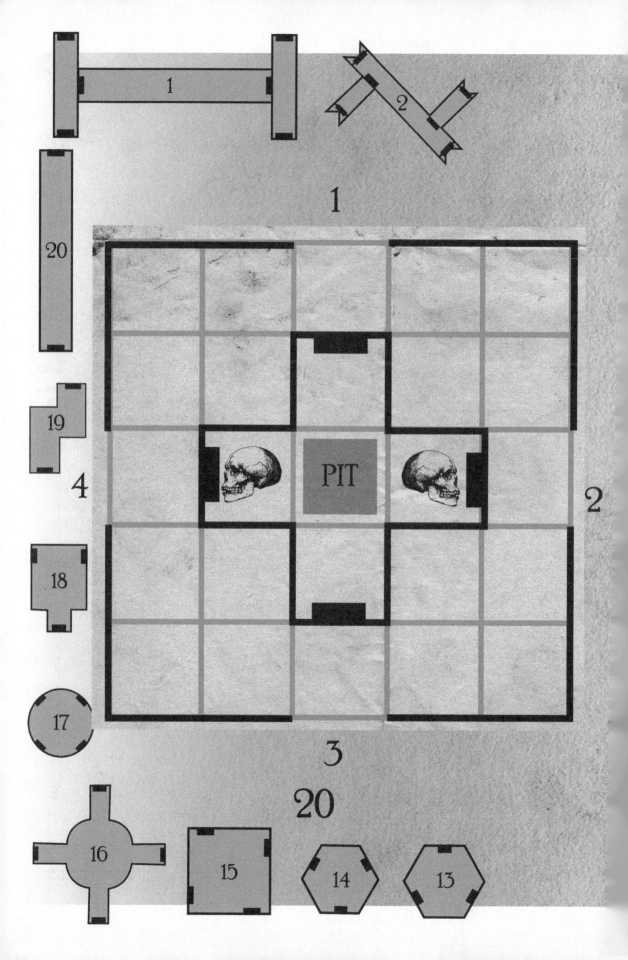

1

2

20

4

2

PIT

3

20

17   16   15   14   13

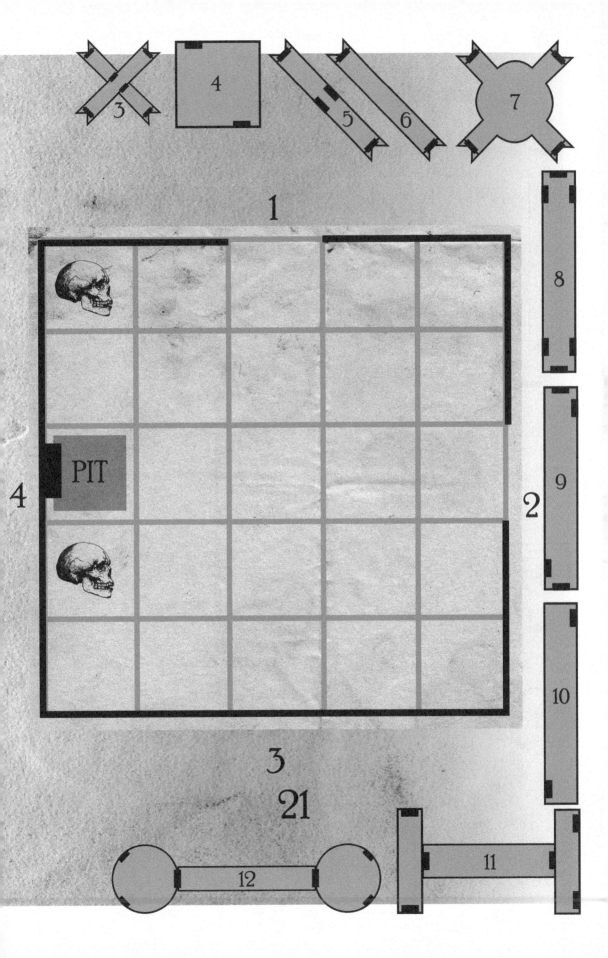

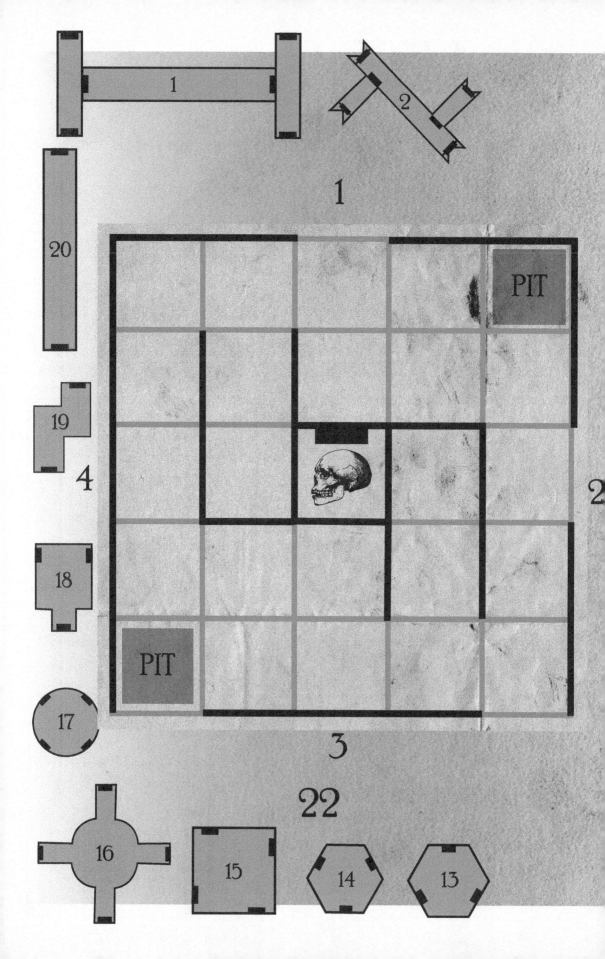

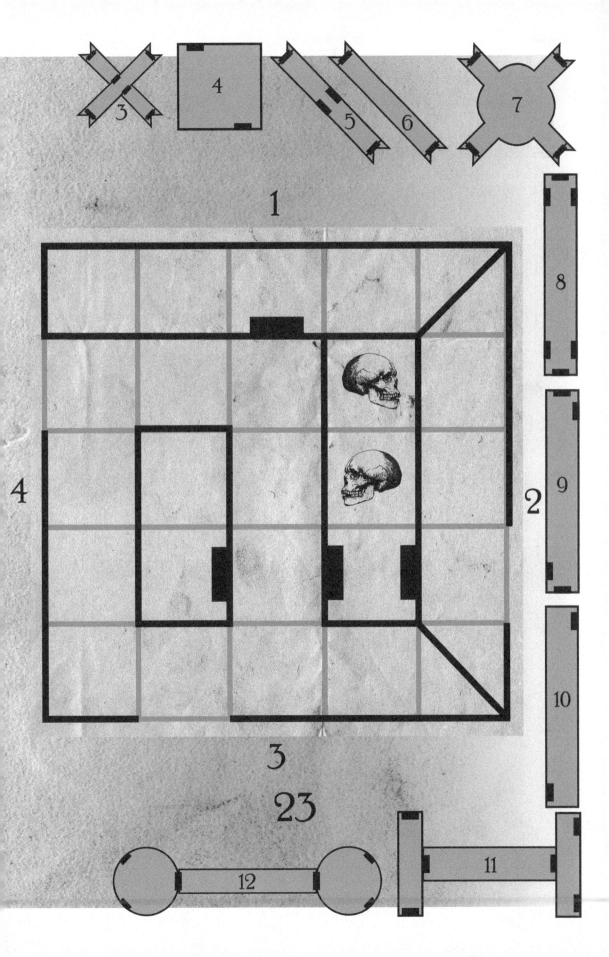

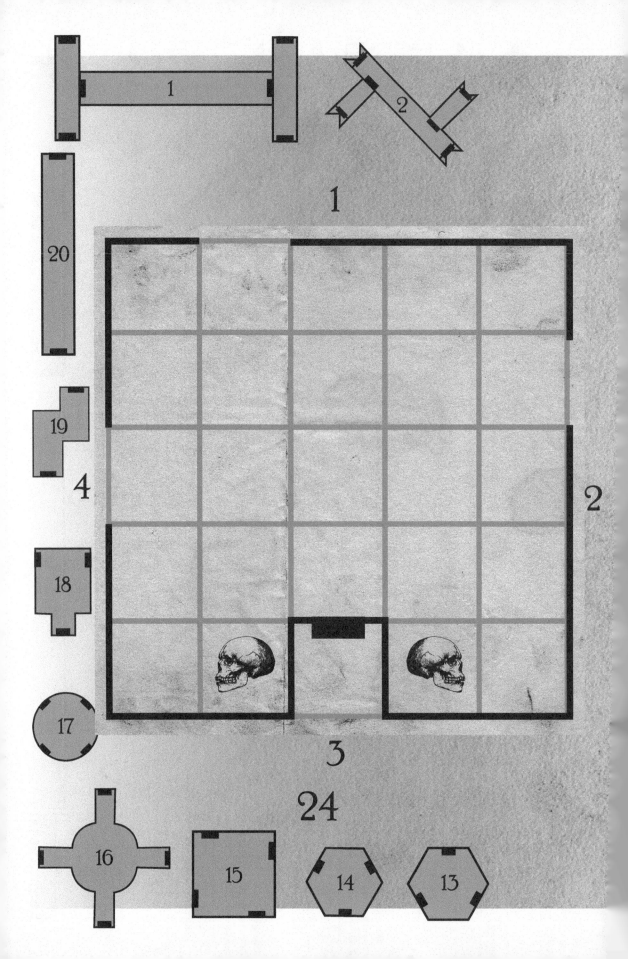

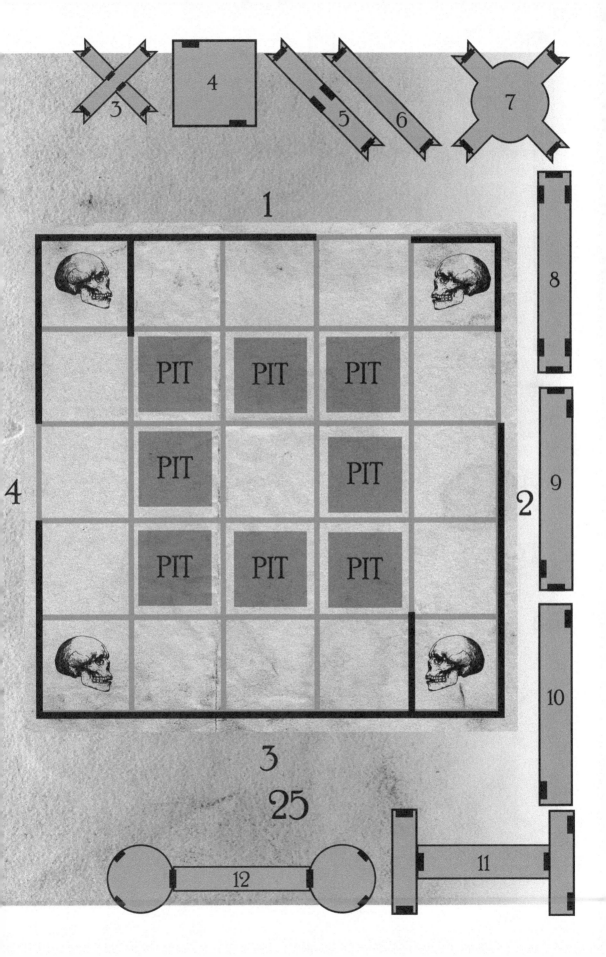

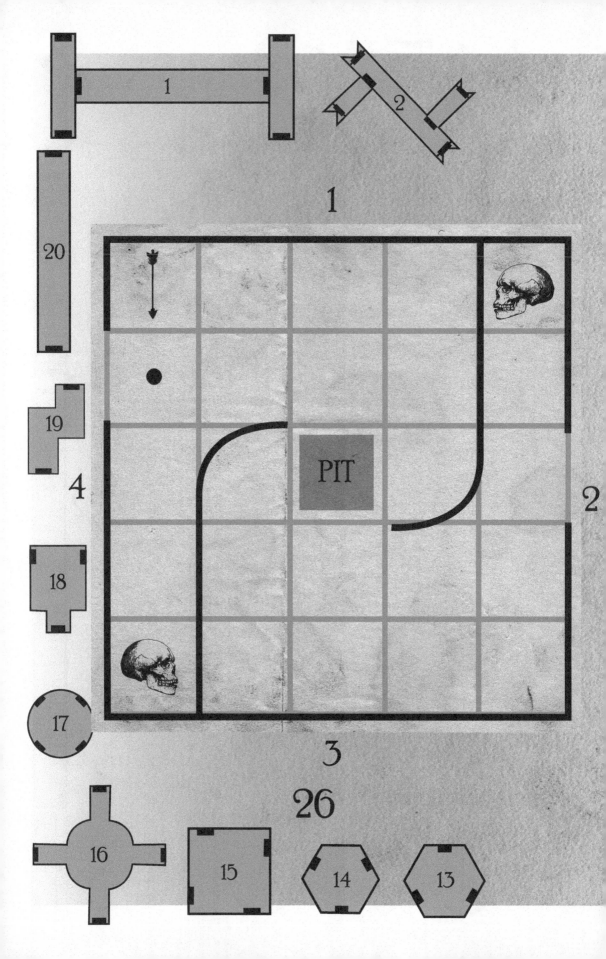

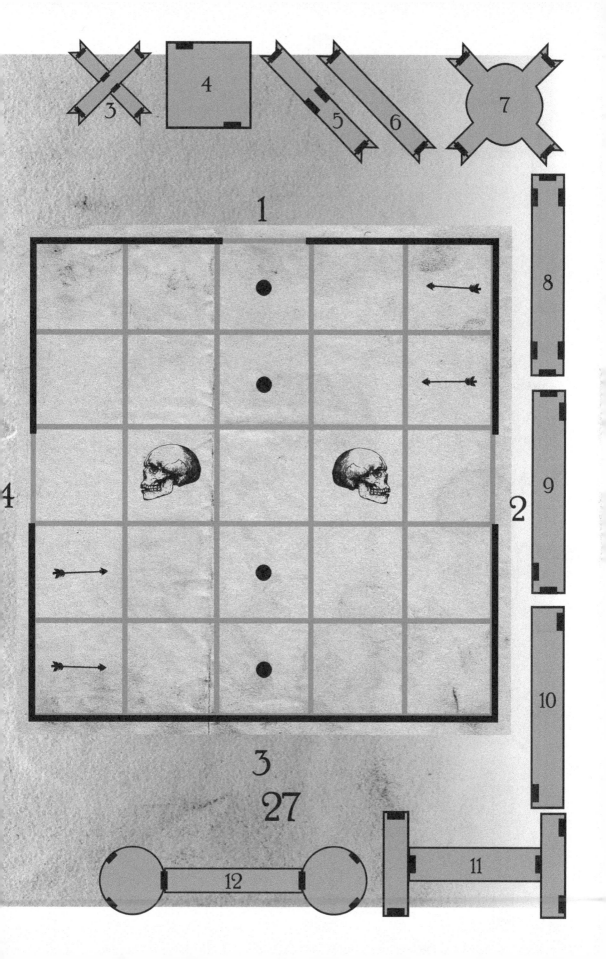

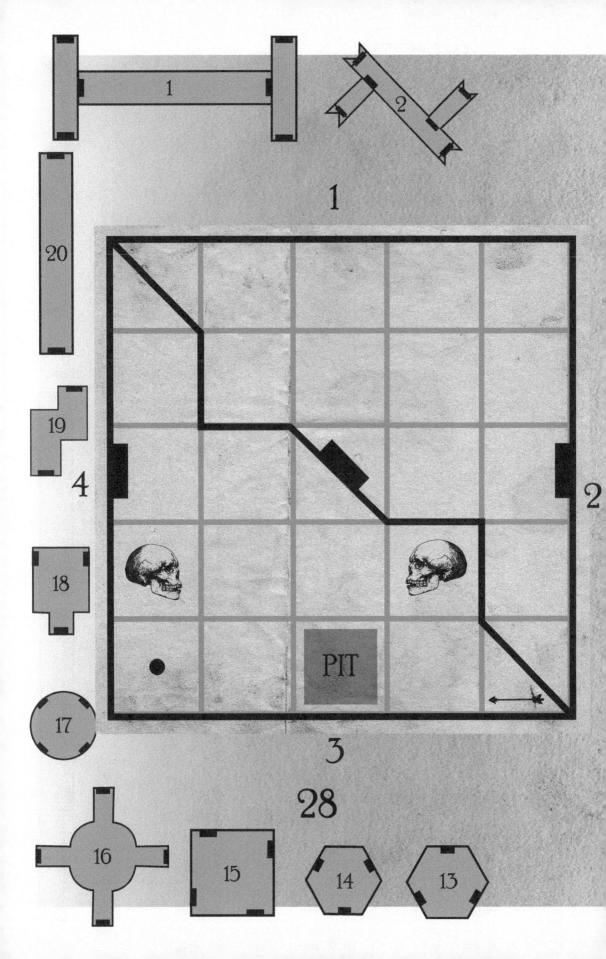

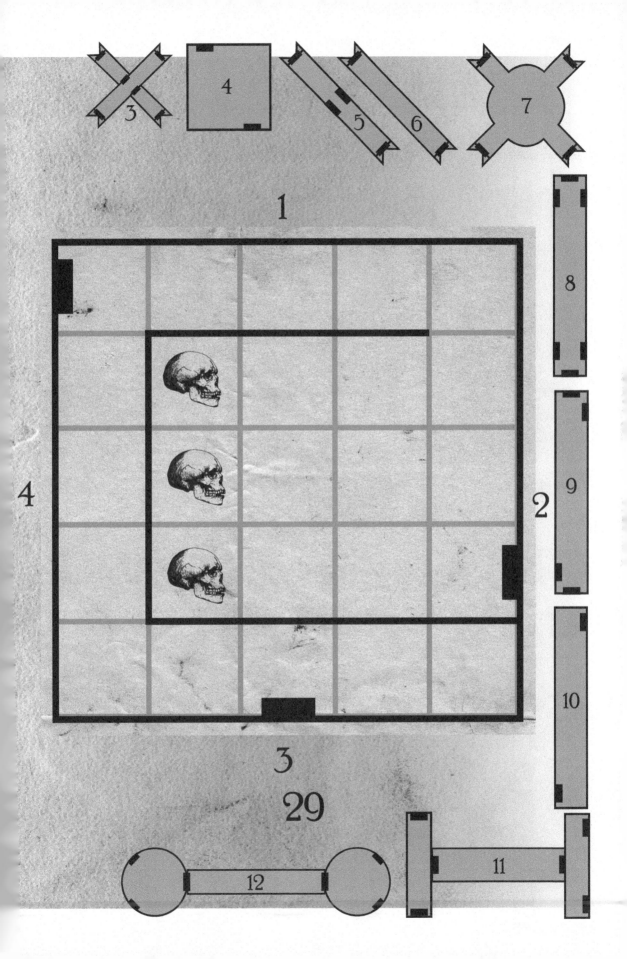

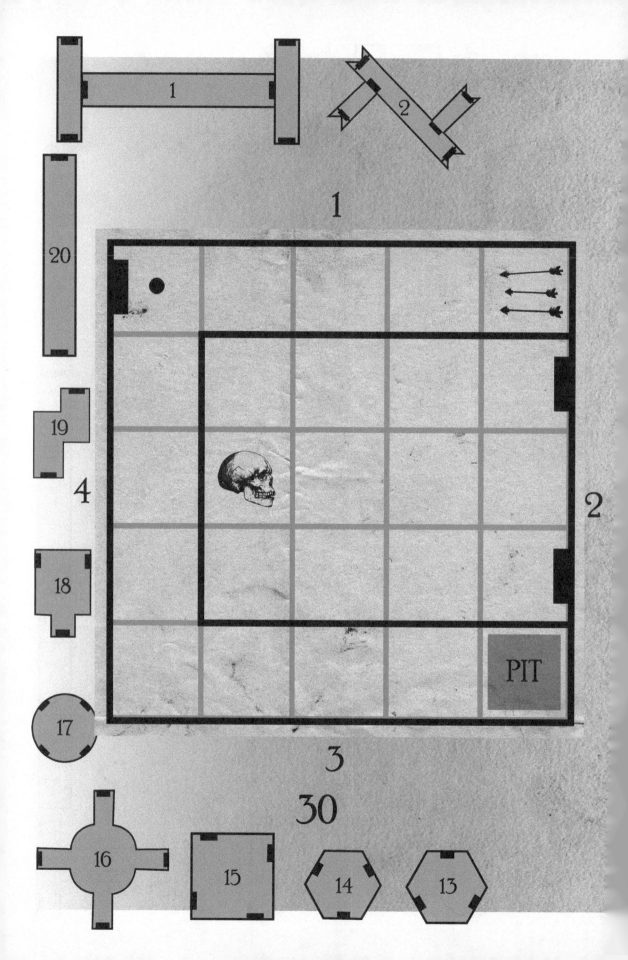

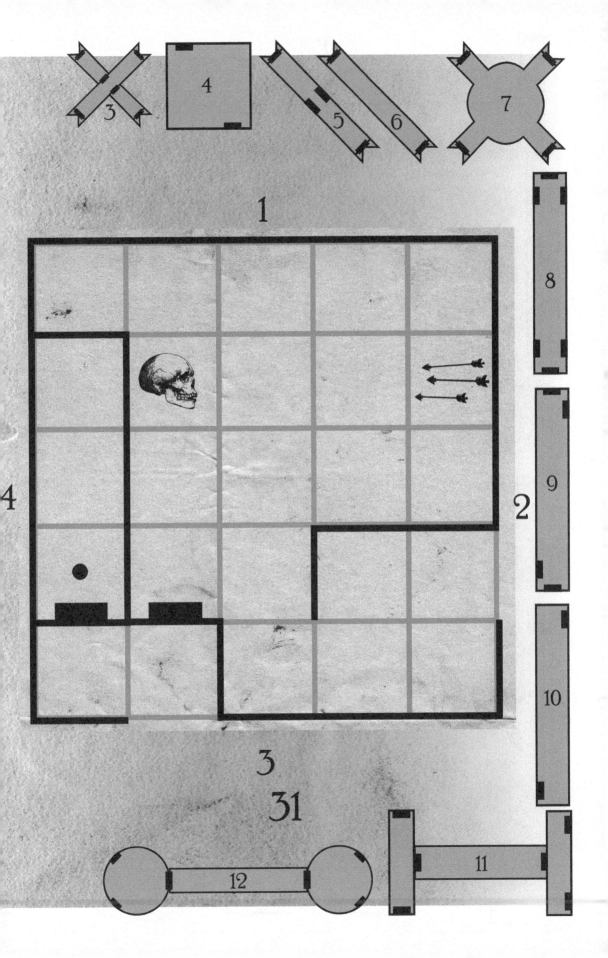

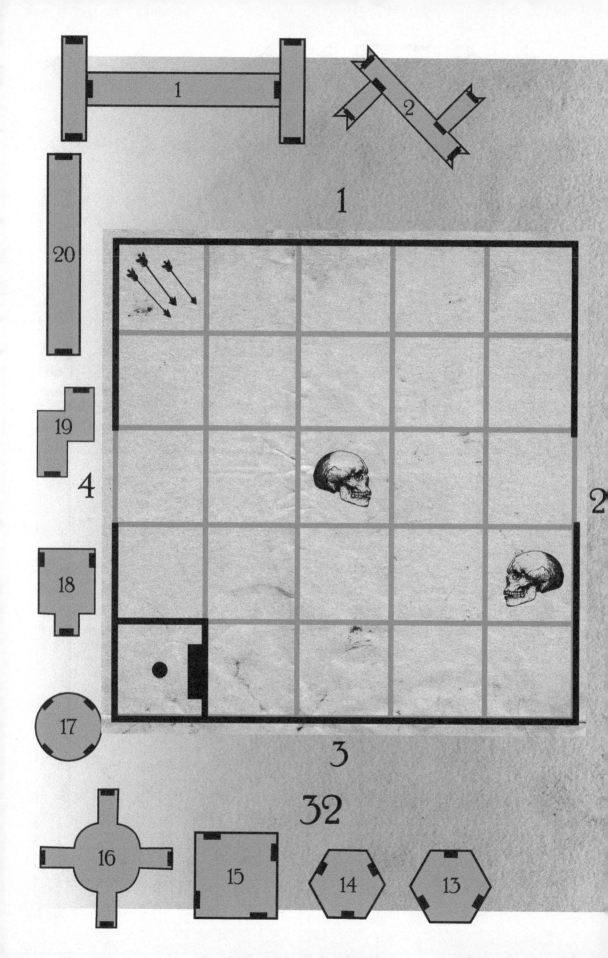

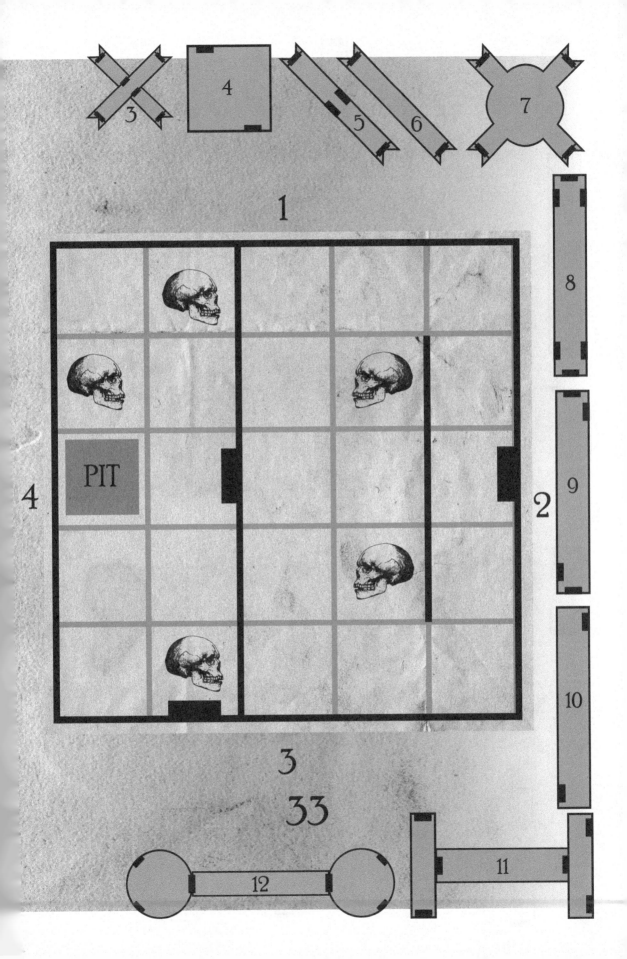

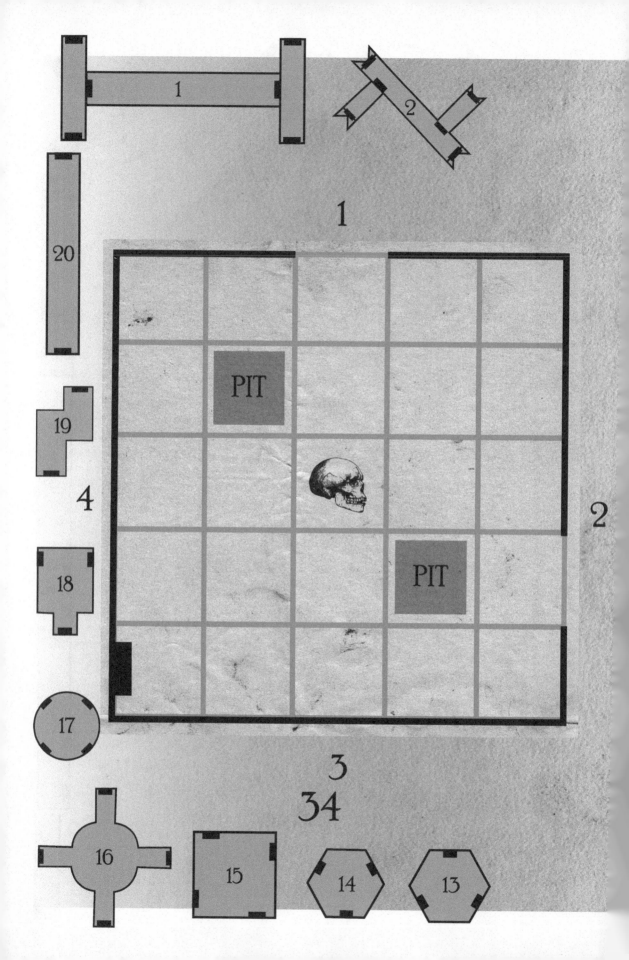

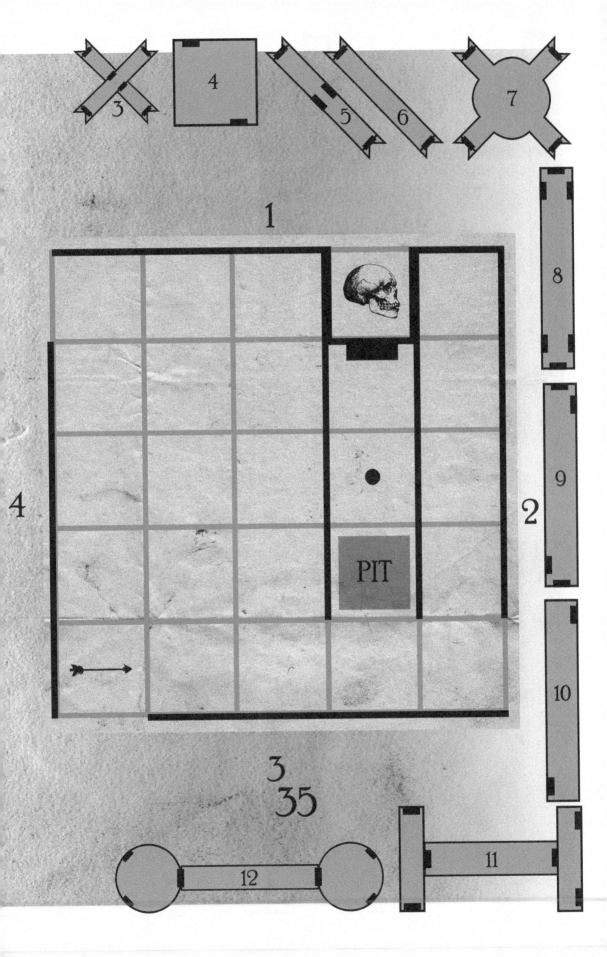

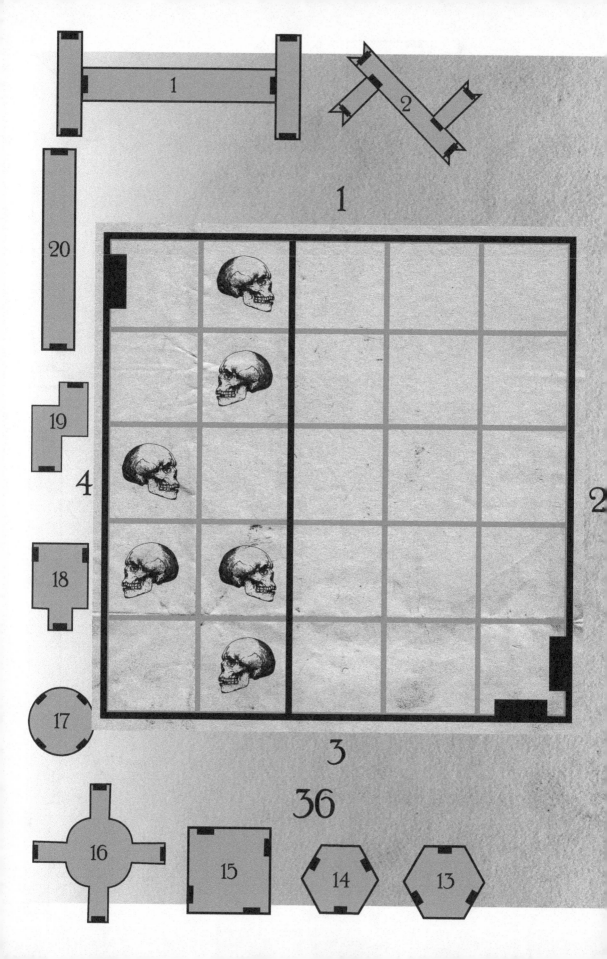

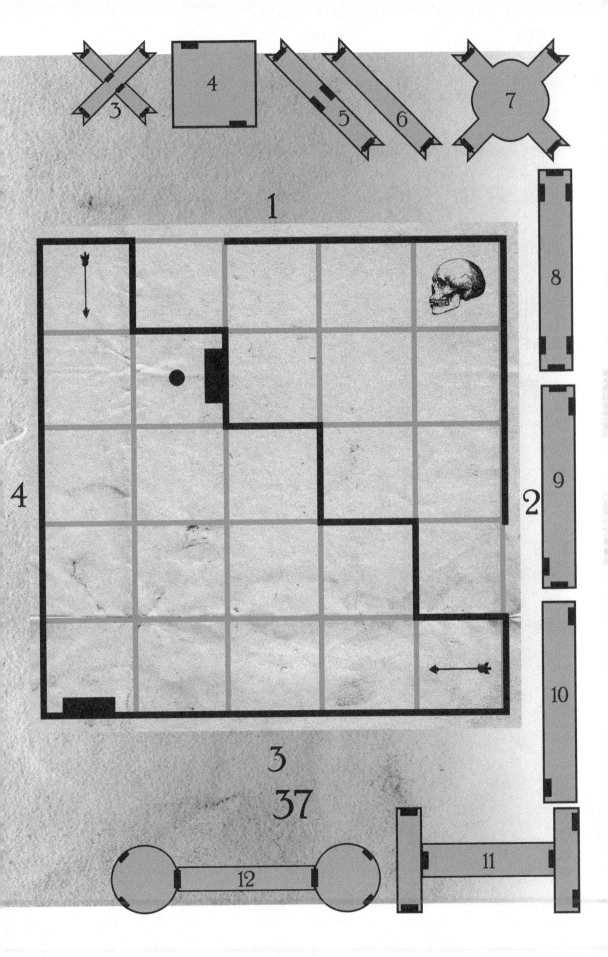

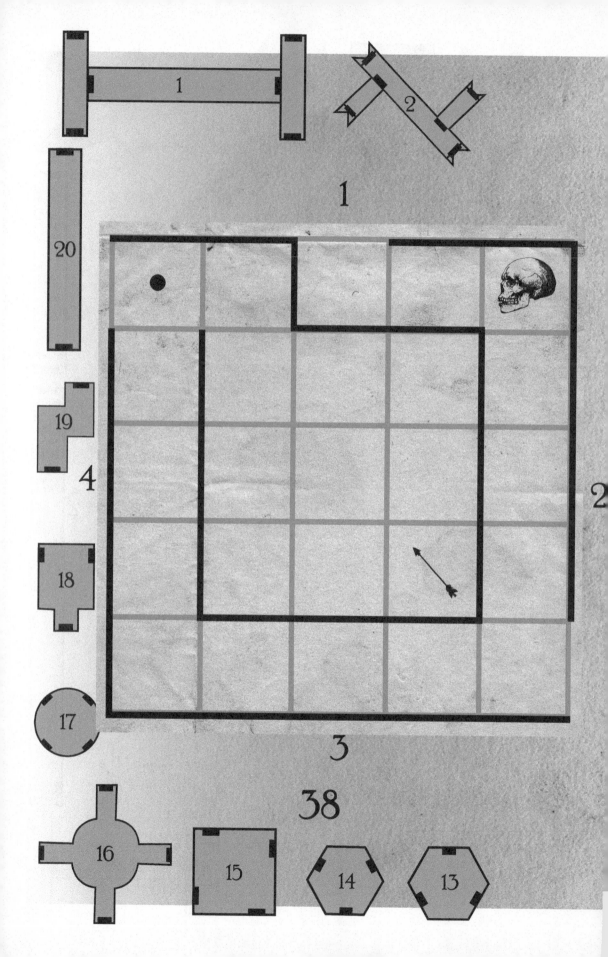

1

20

4

19

18

17

3

38

16   15   14   13

1

2

2

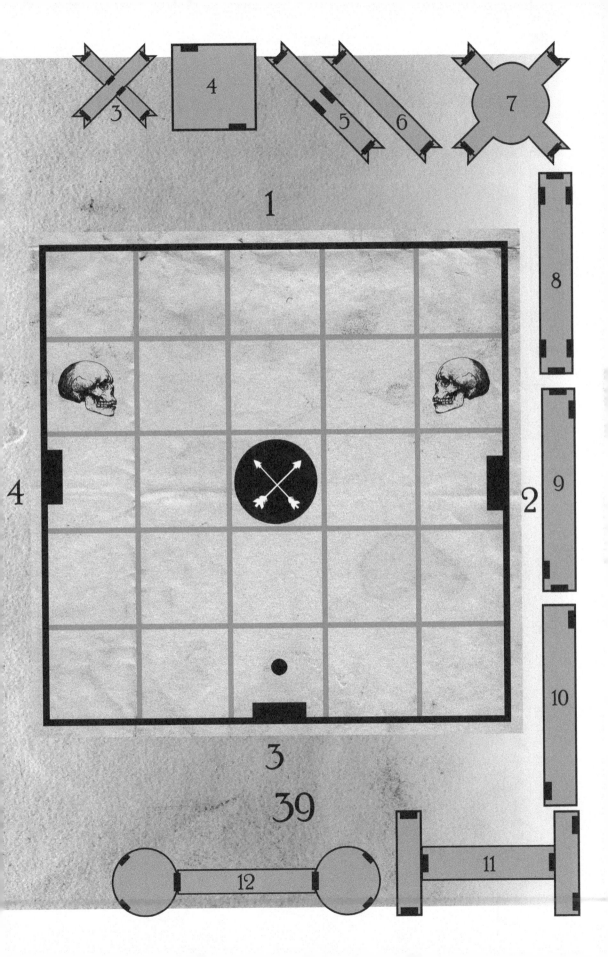

1

3

4

5

6

7

8

4

2

9

10

3

39

12

11

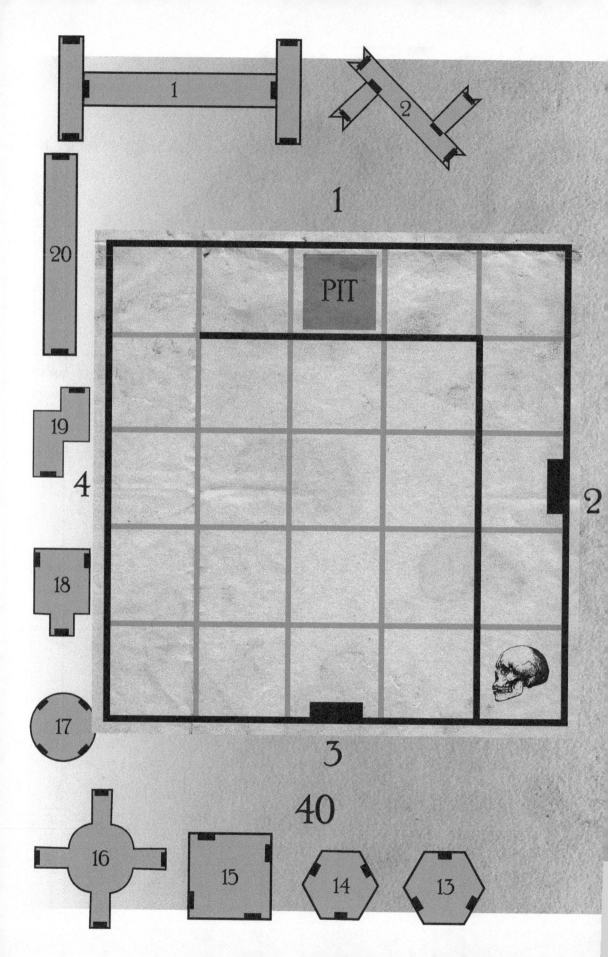

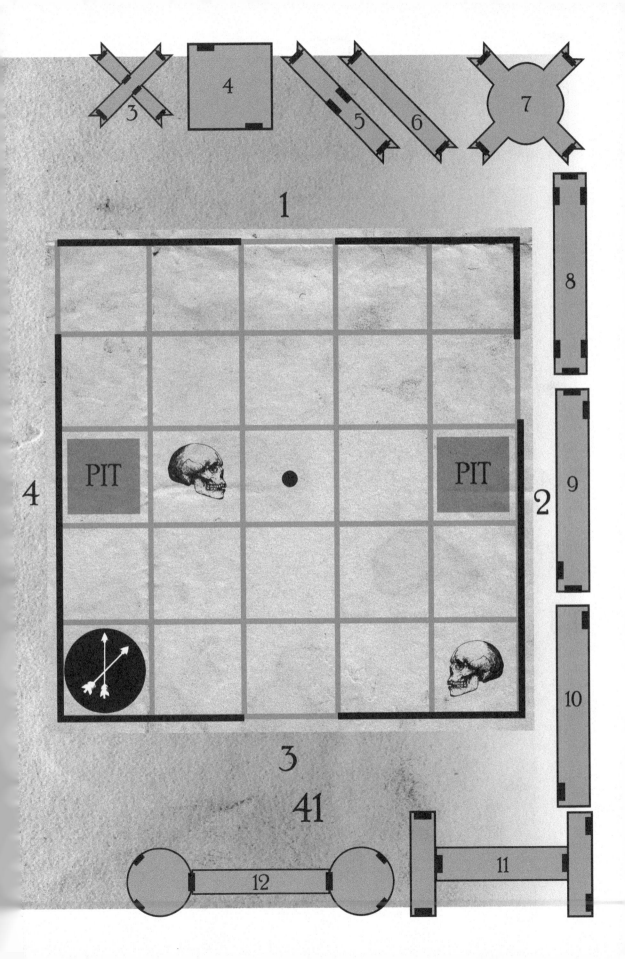

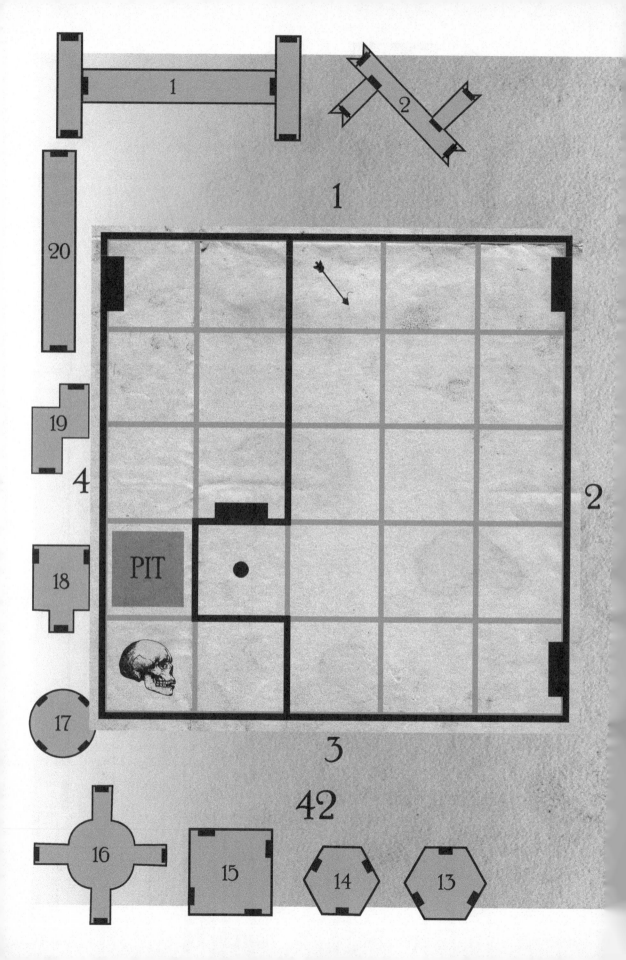

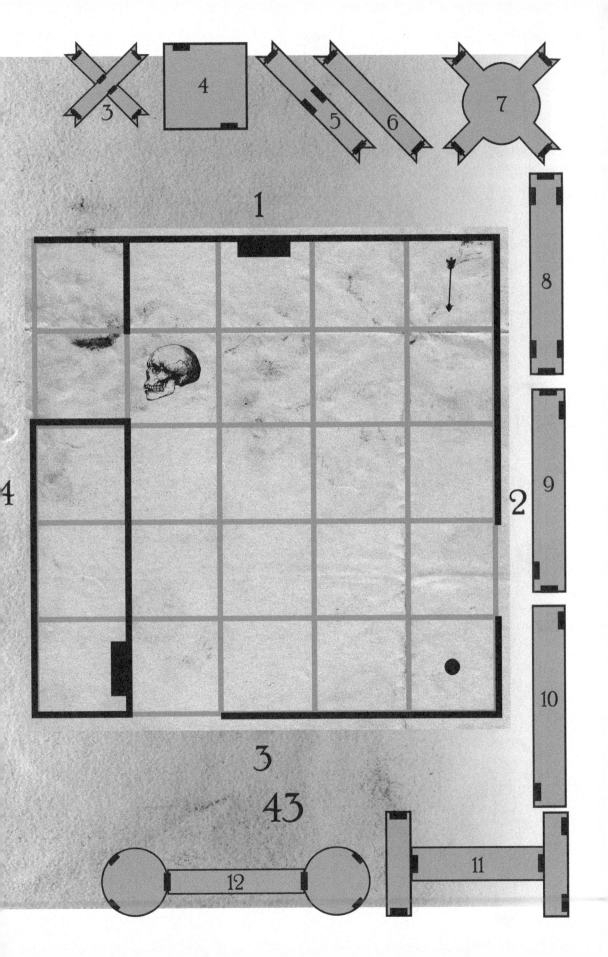

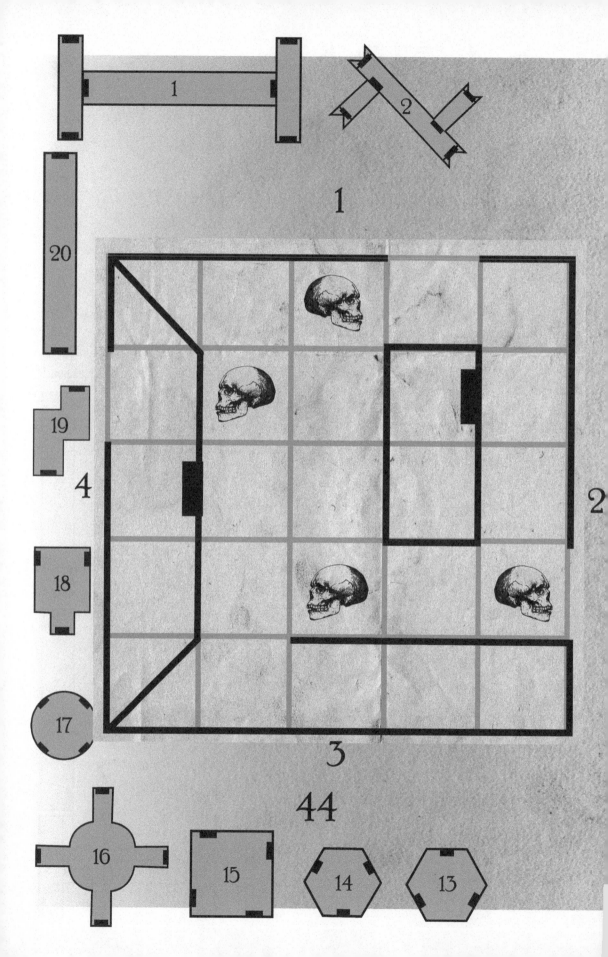

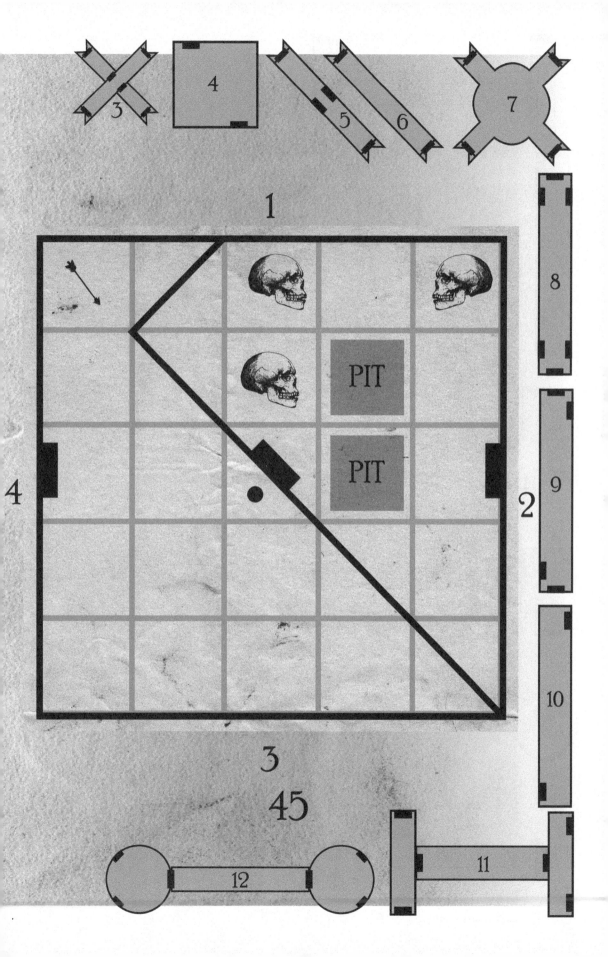

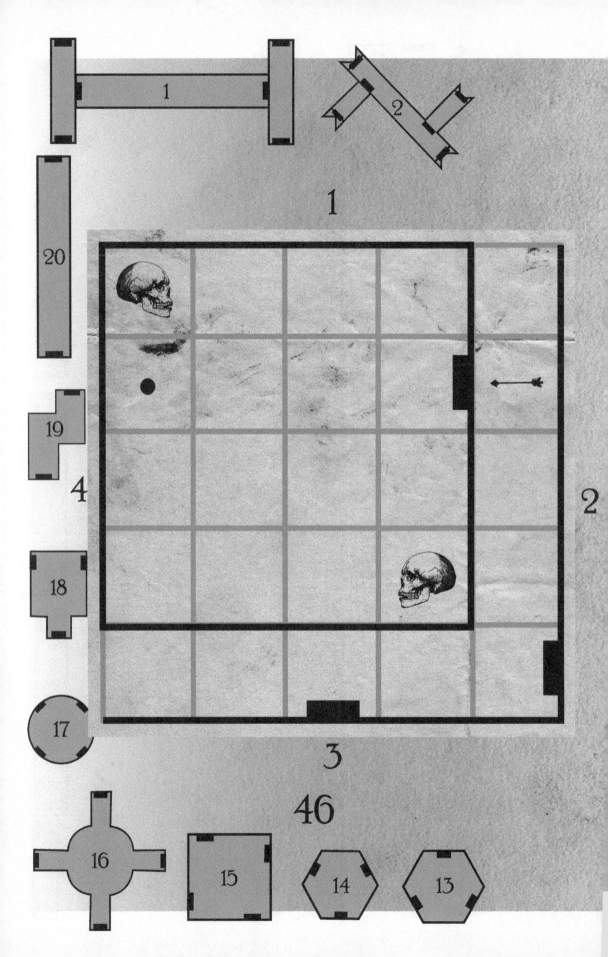

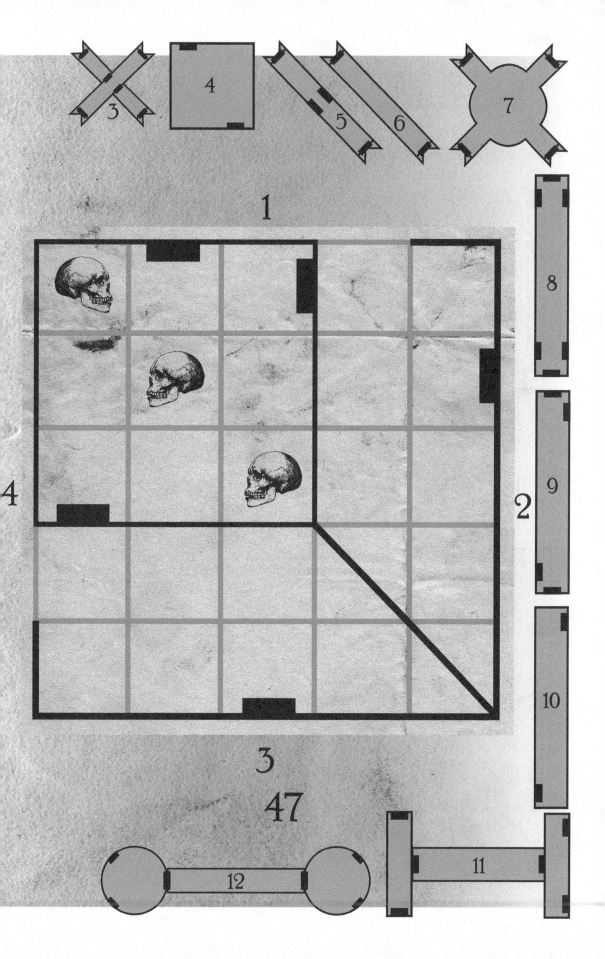

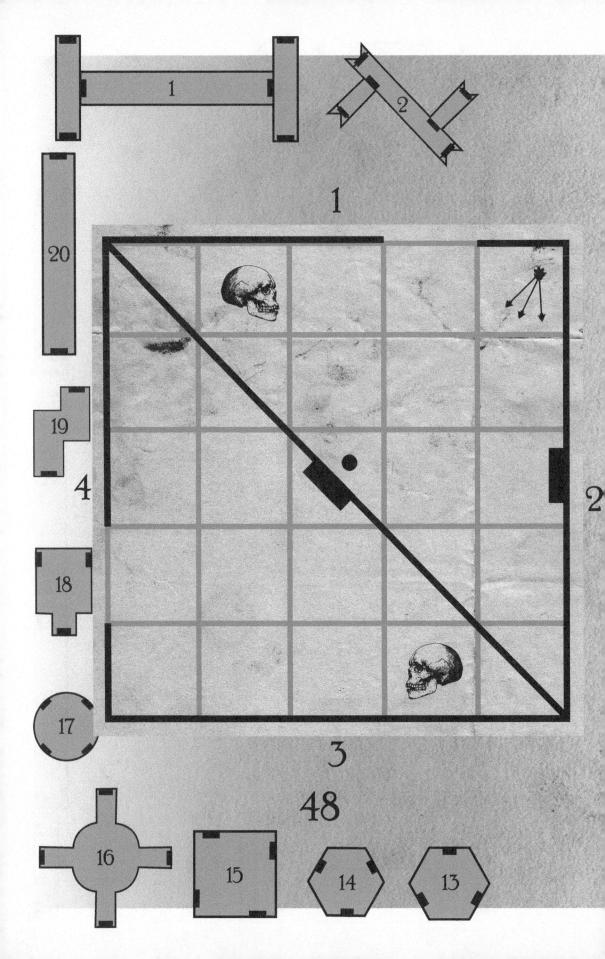

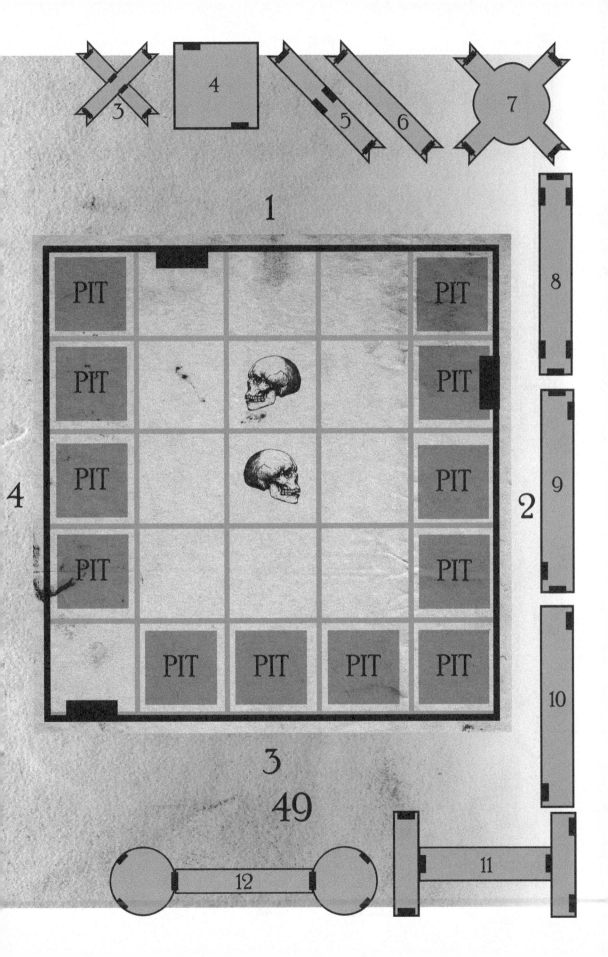

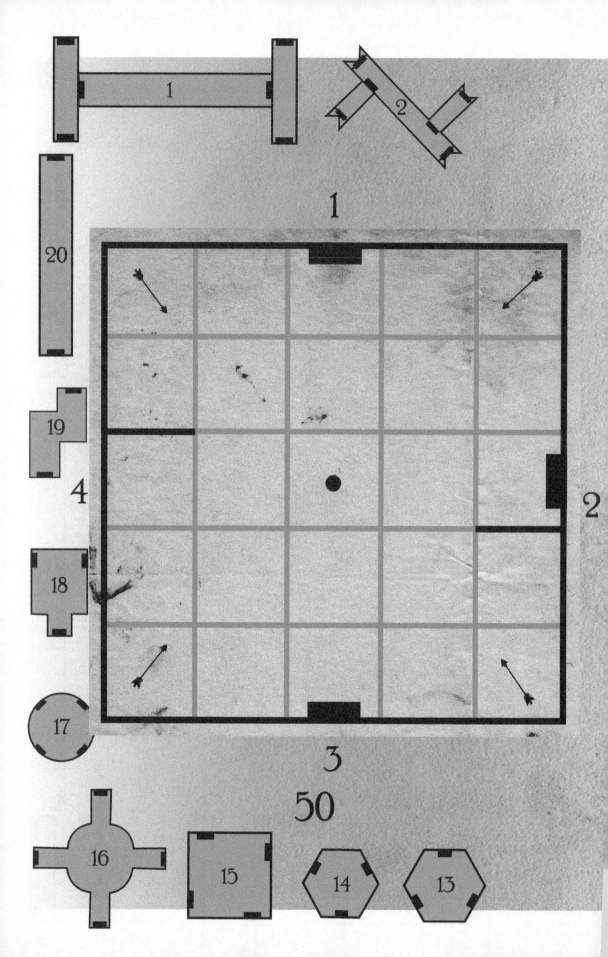

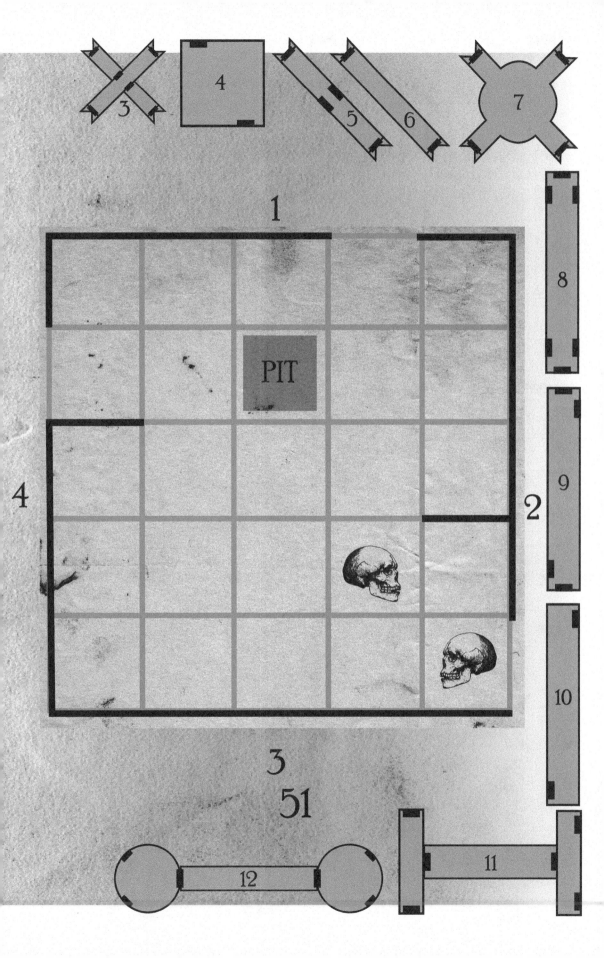

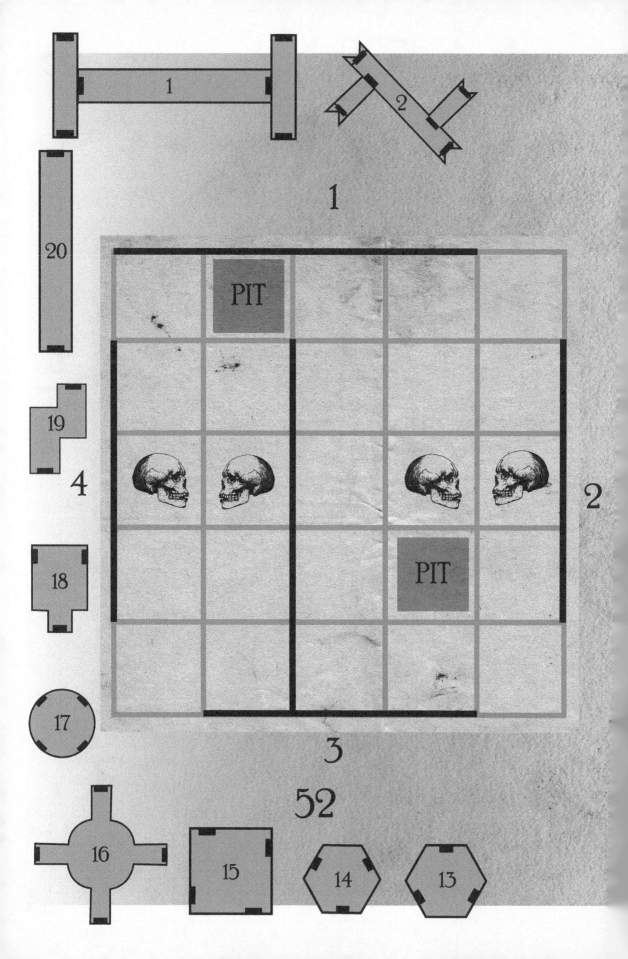

52

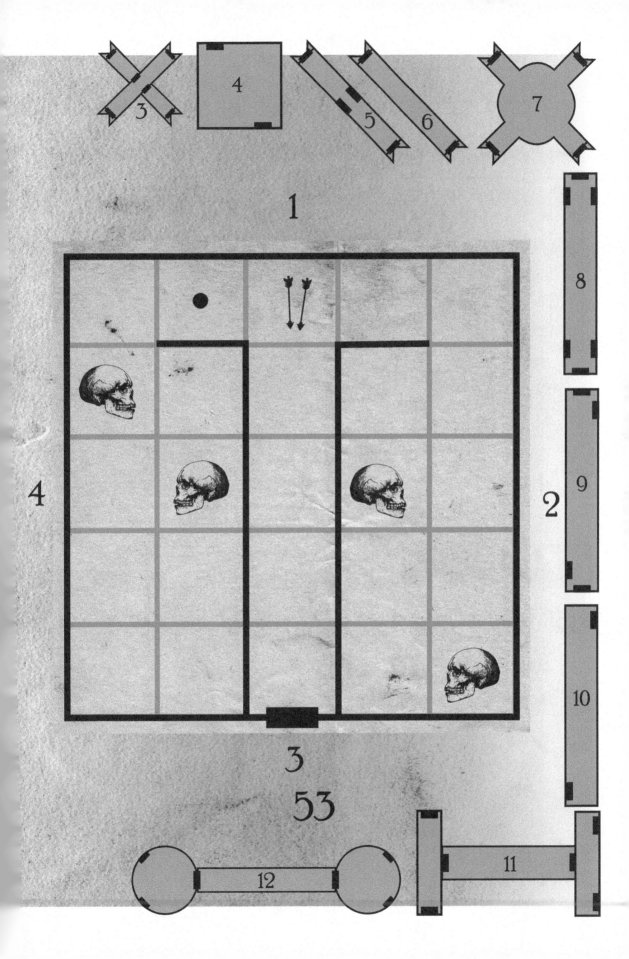

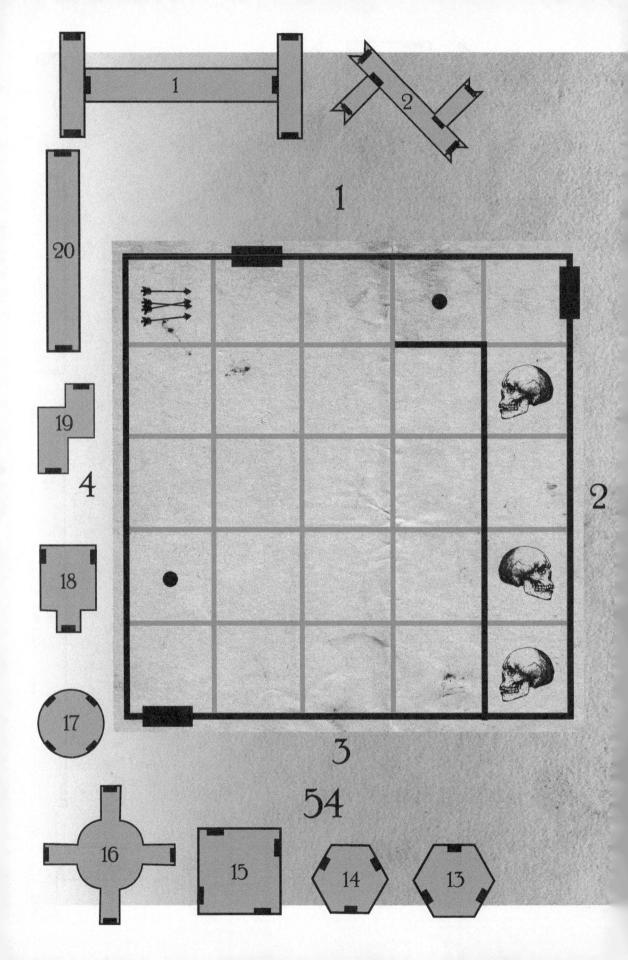

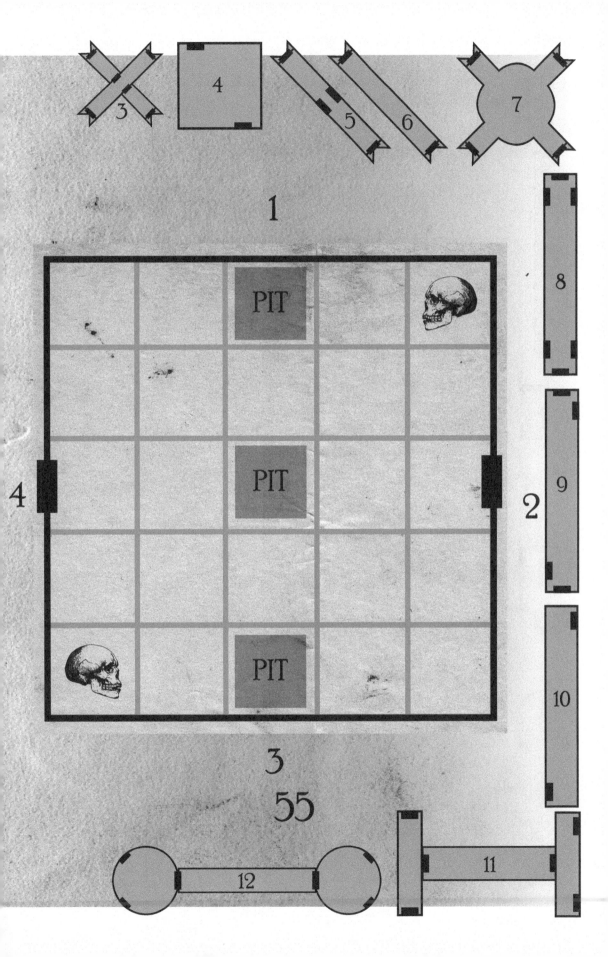

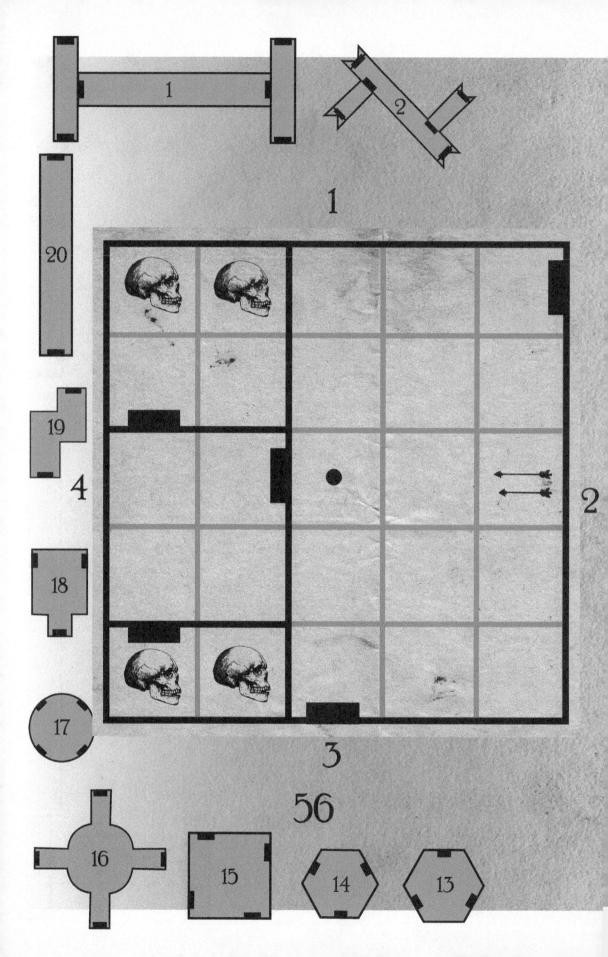

56

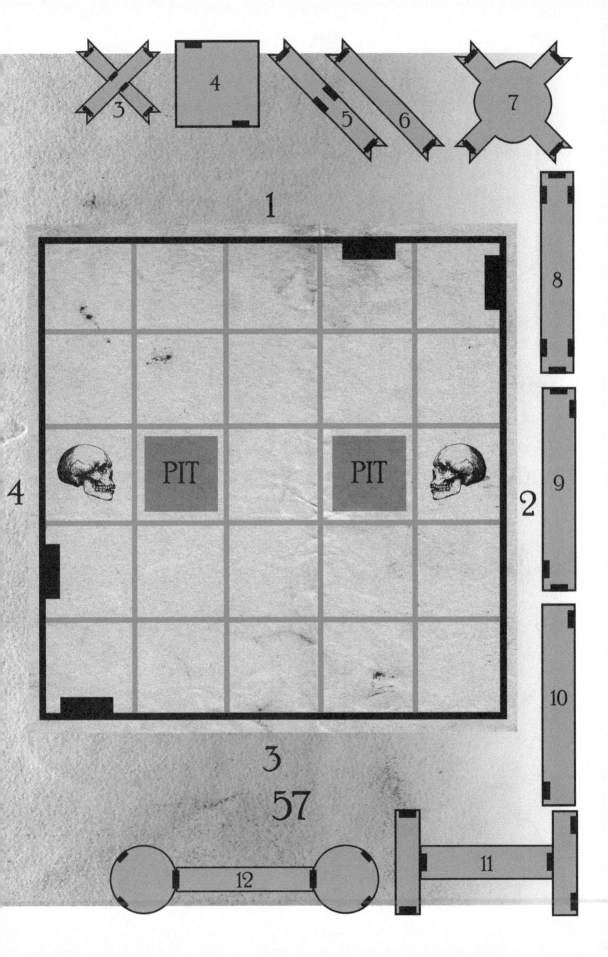

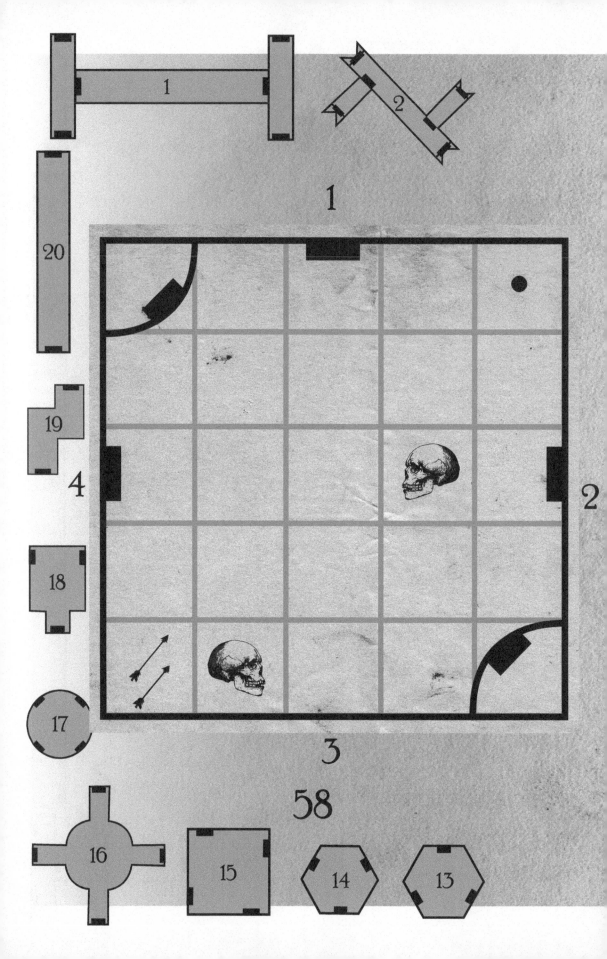

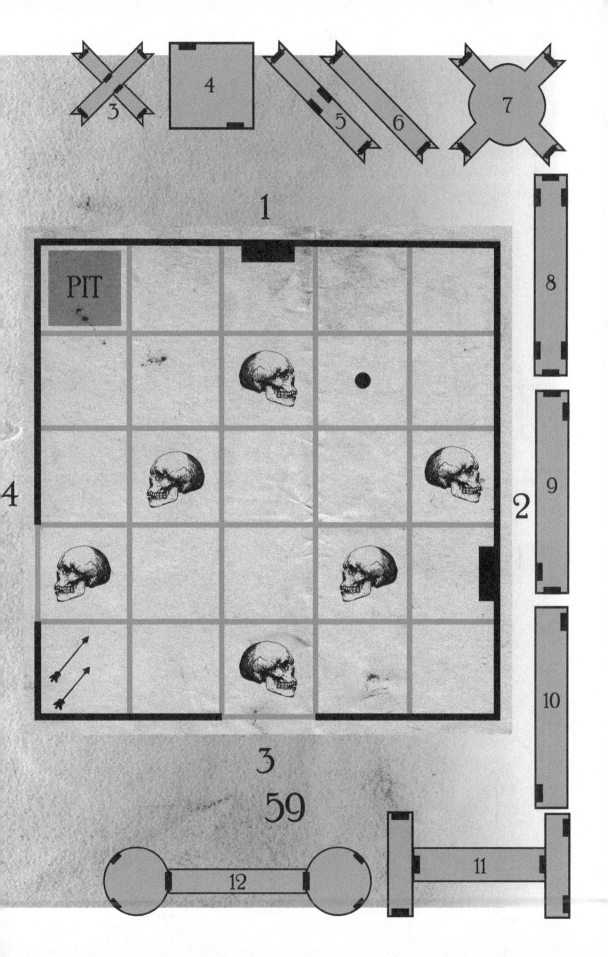

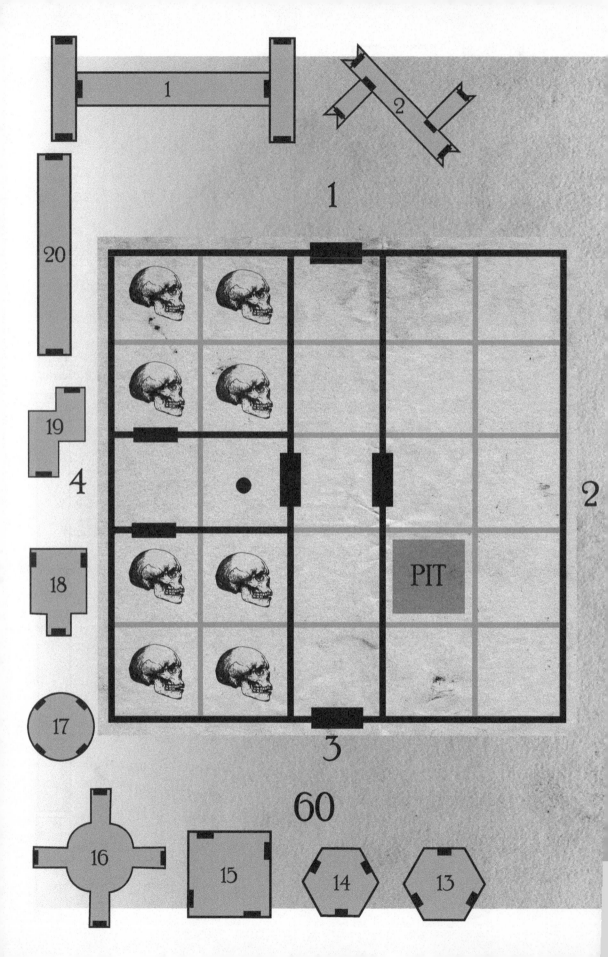

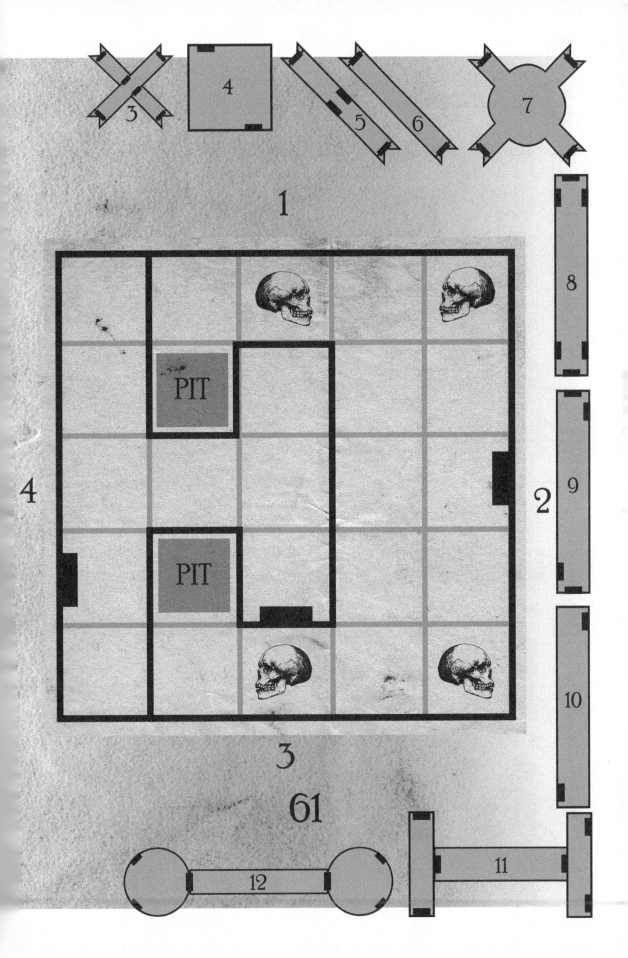

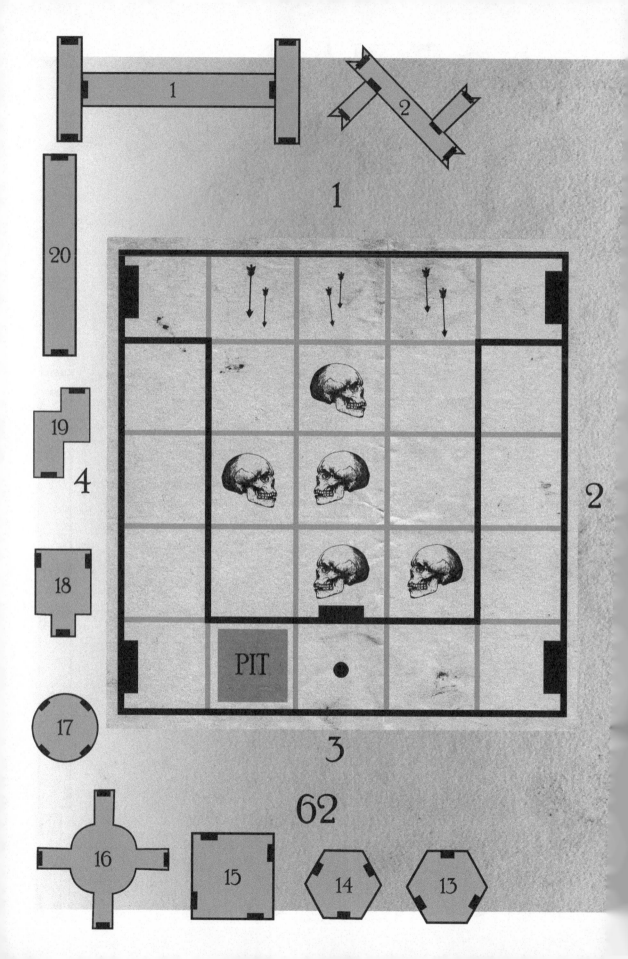

PIT

1

2

3

4

62

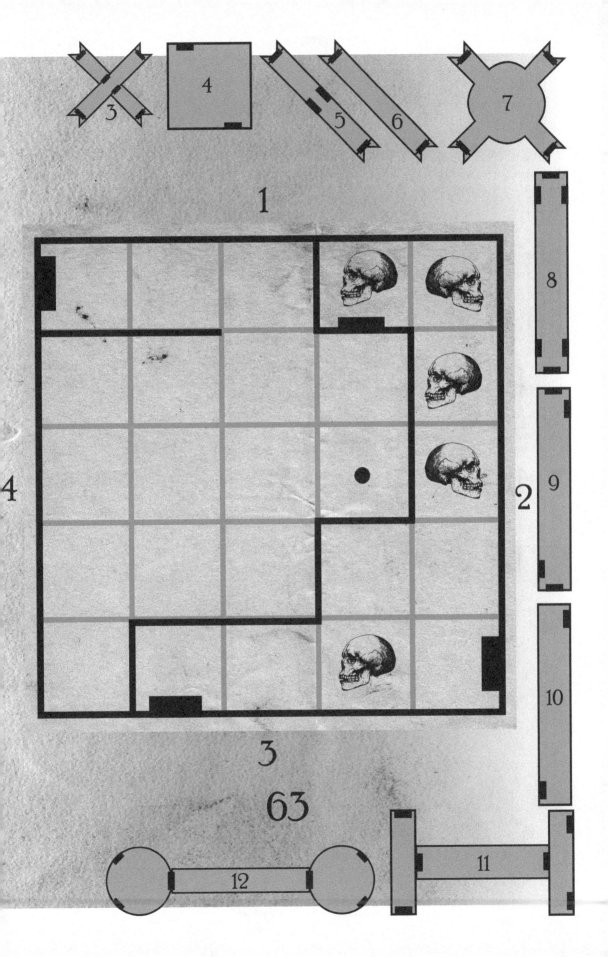

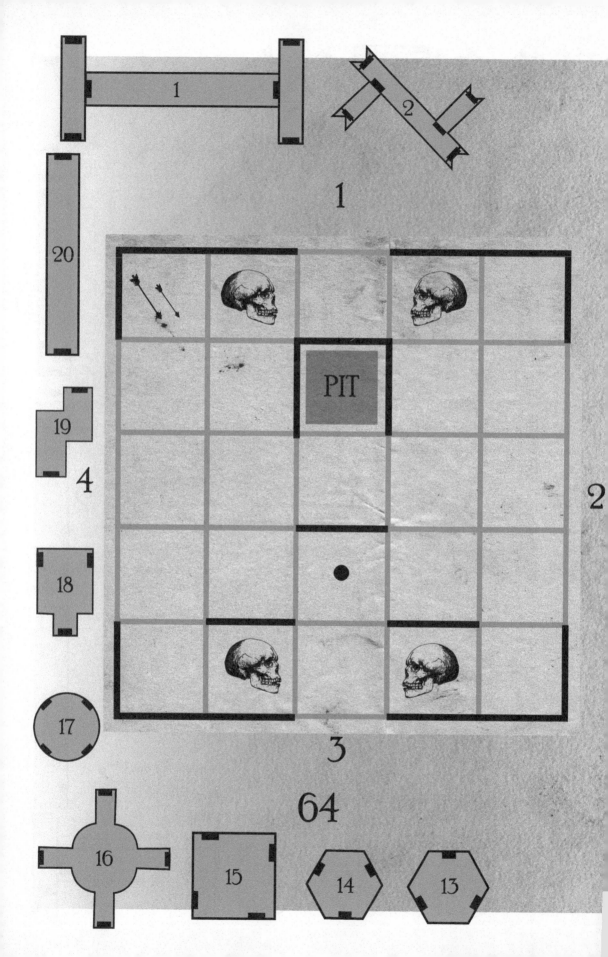

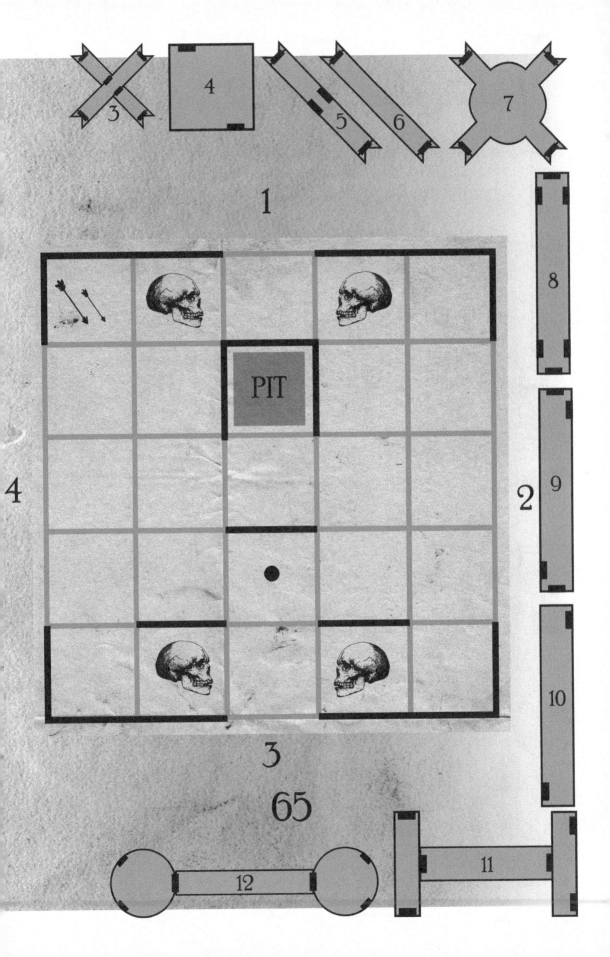

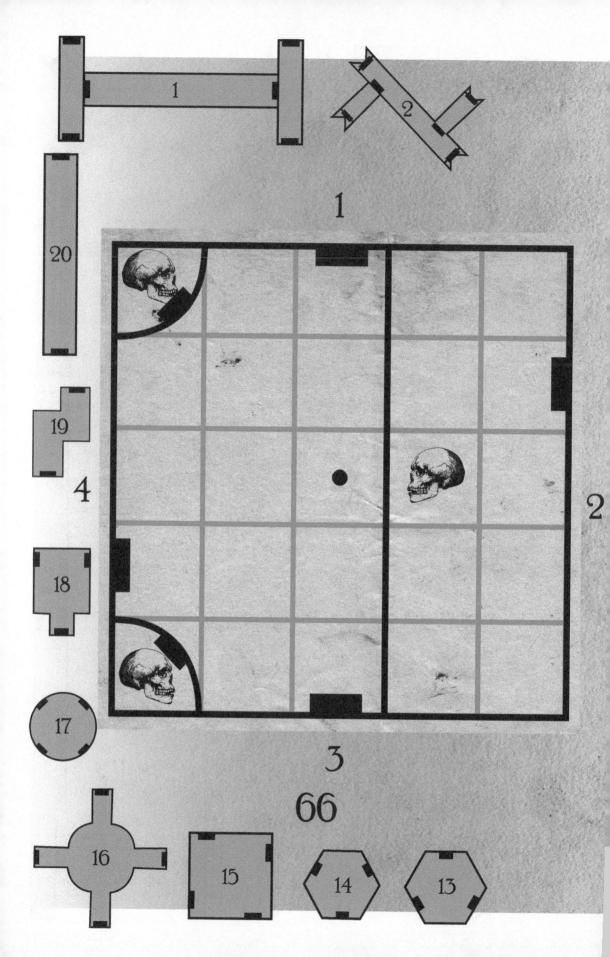

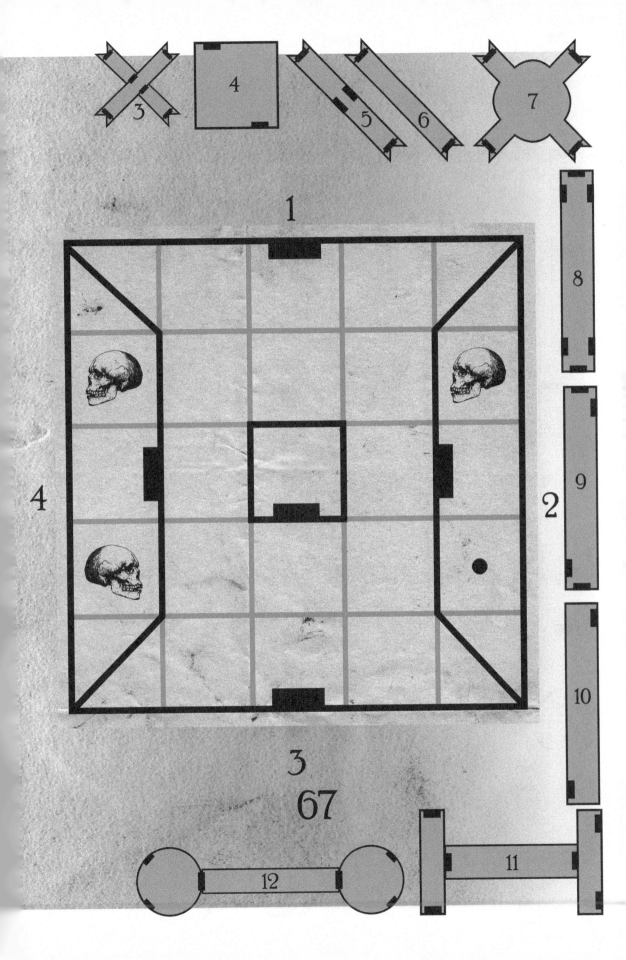

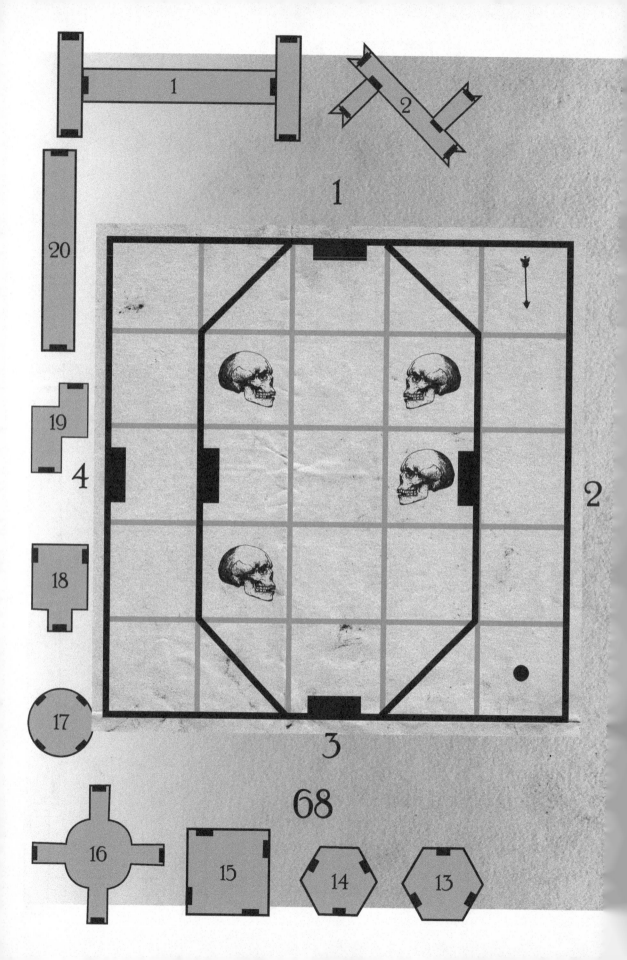

68

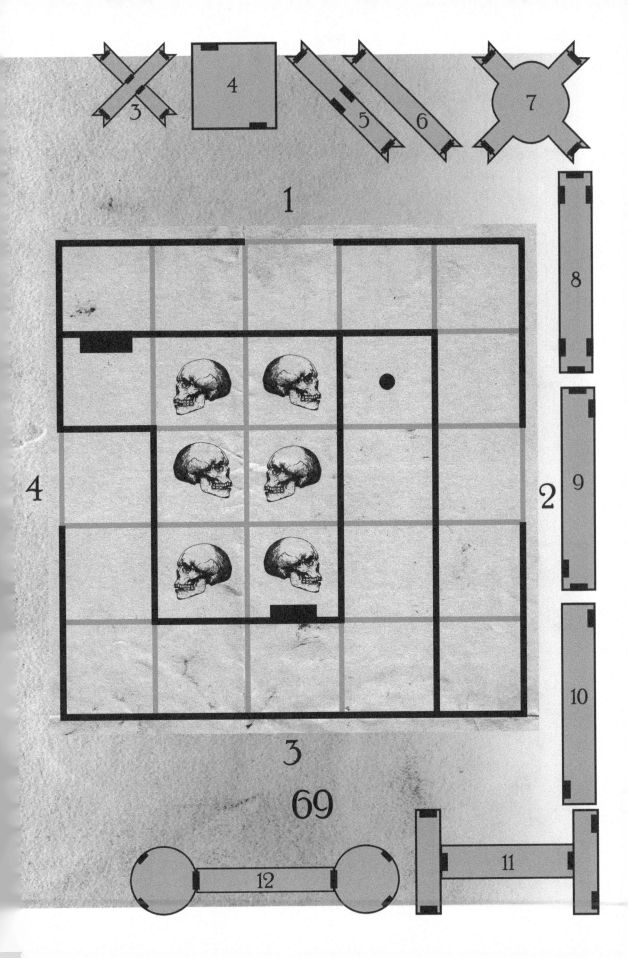

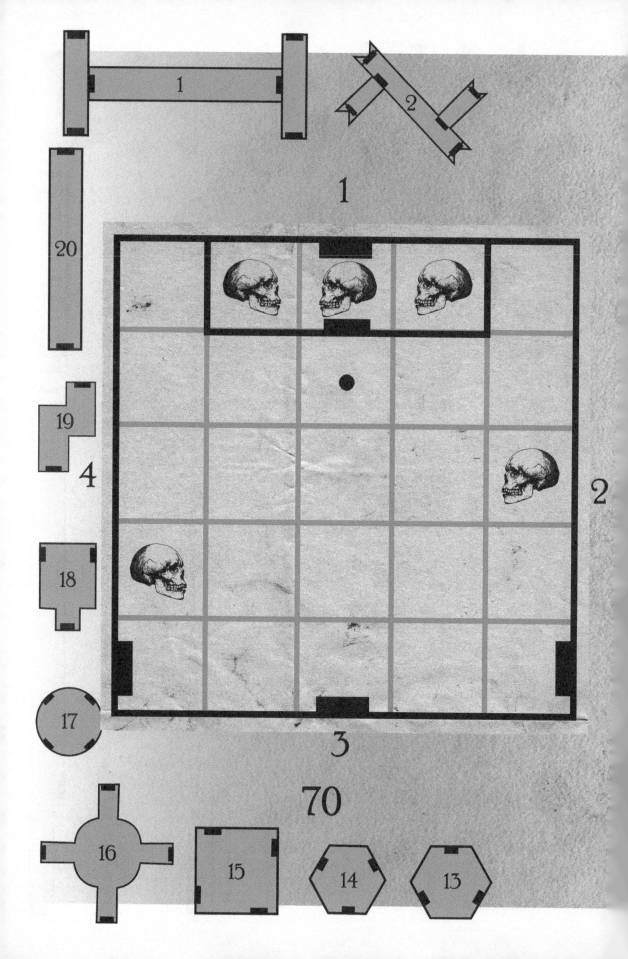

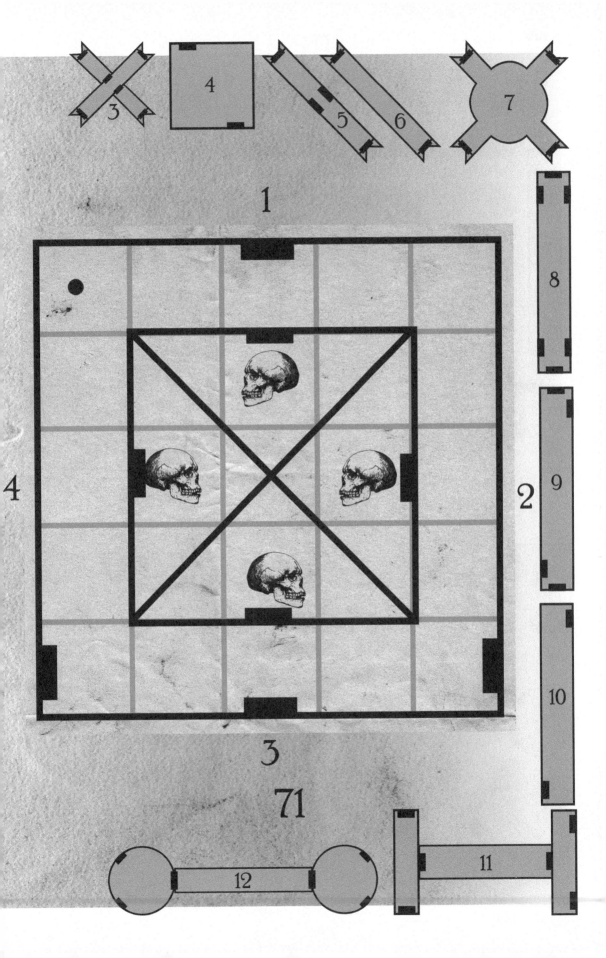

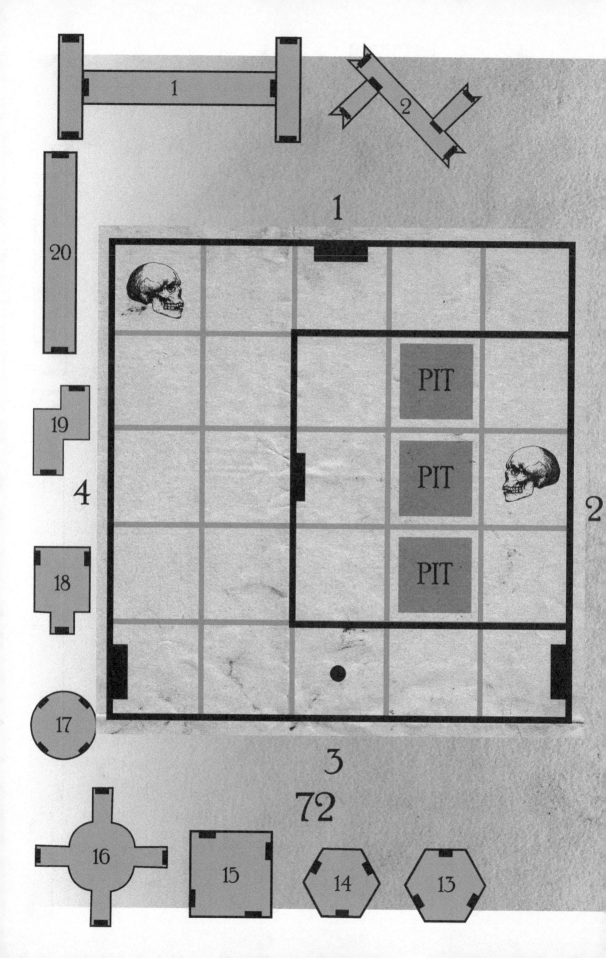

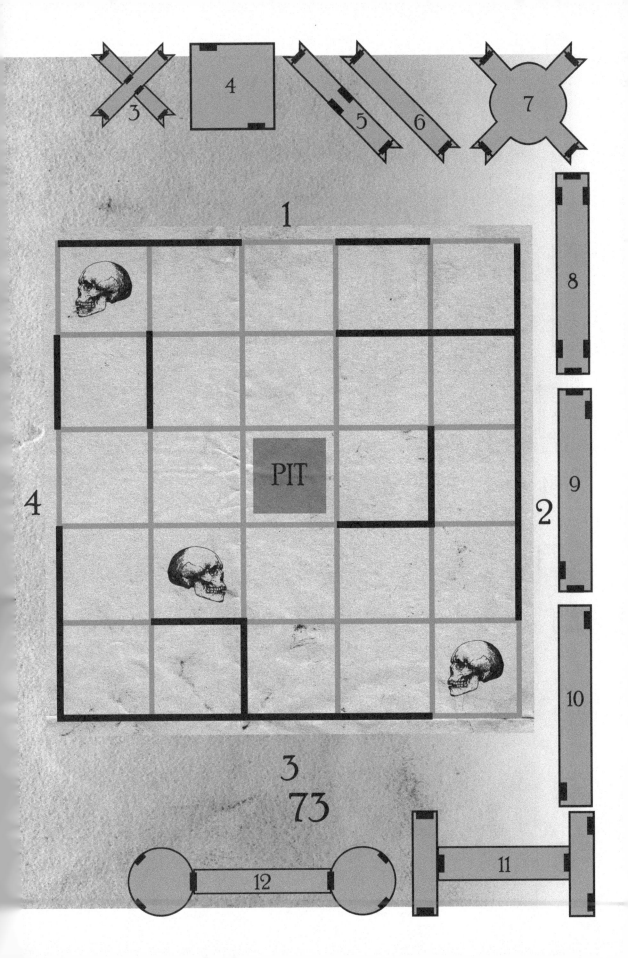

73

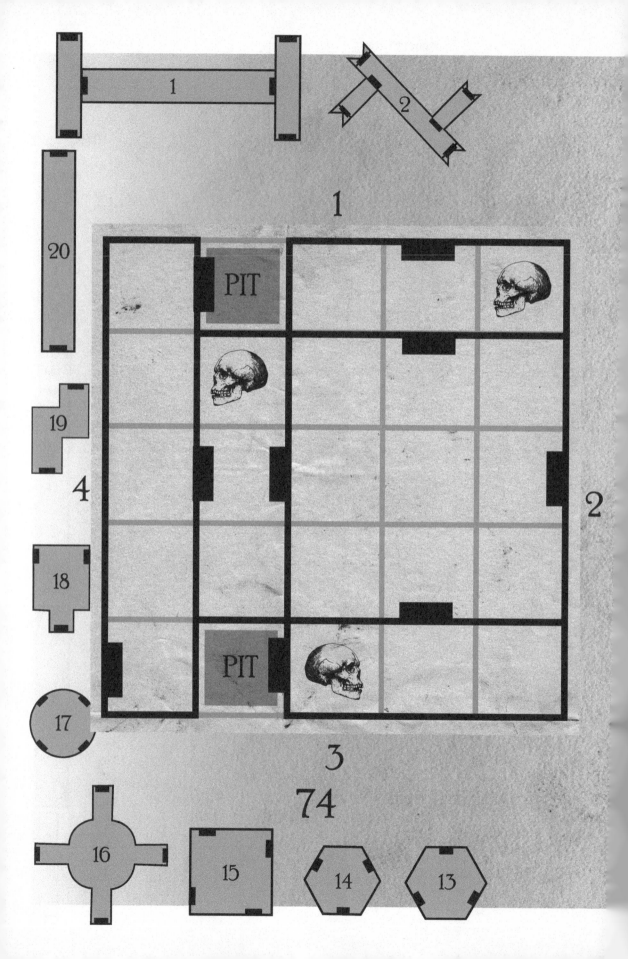

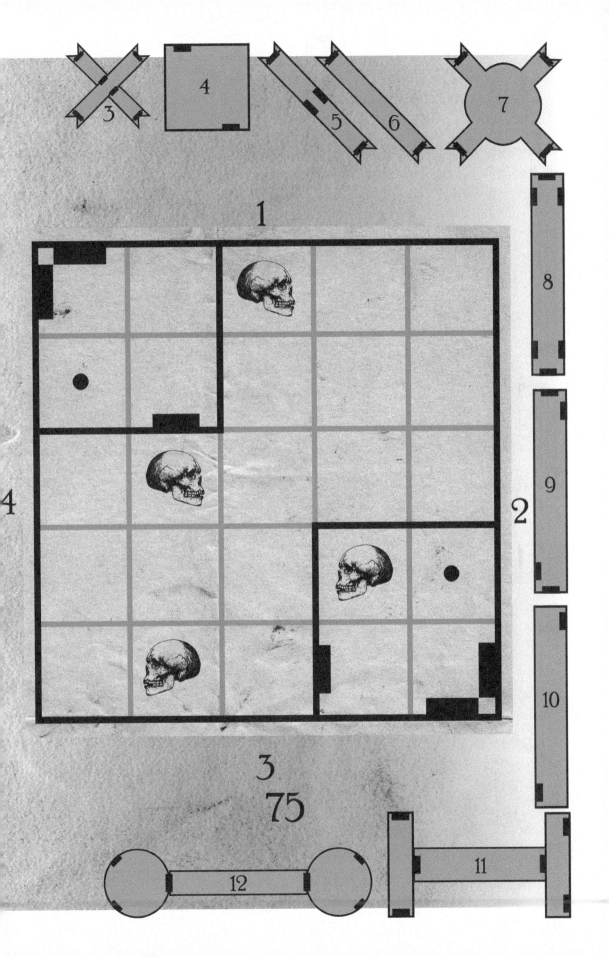

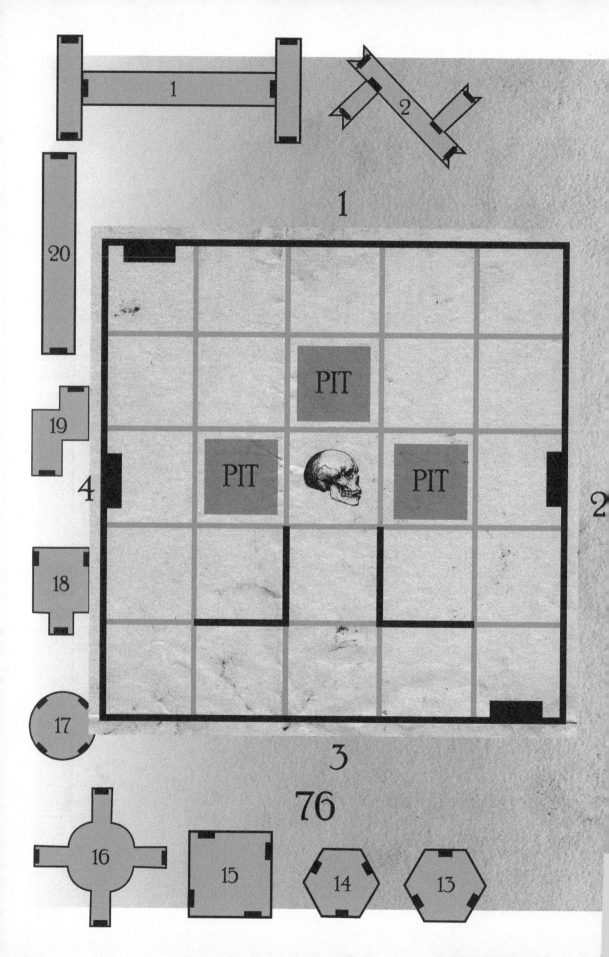

1

2

20

19

4

18

17

PIT

PIT

PIT

2

3

76

16

15

14

13

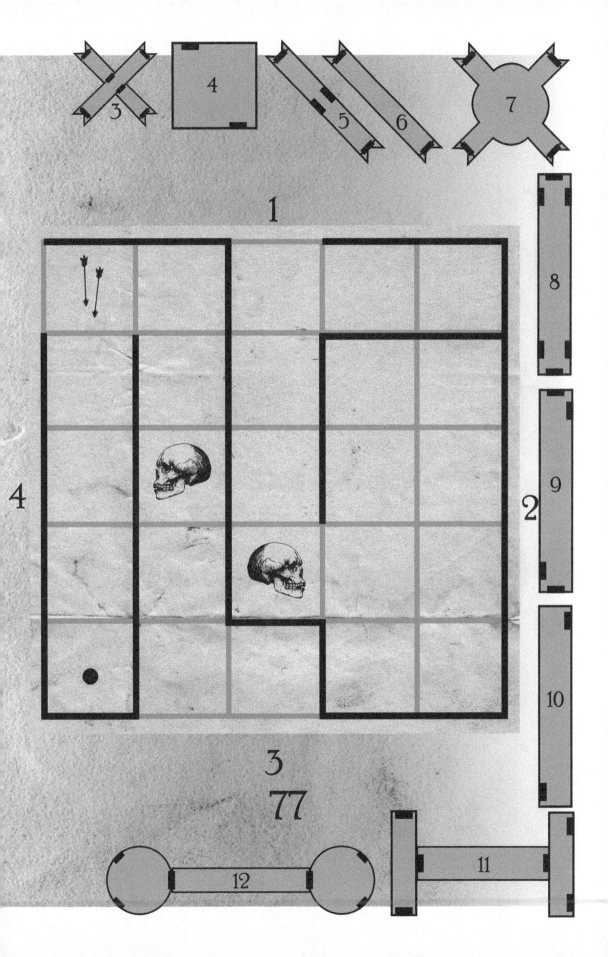

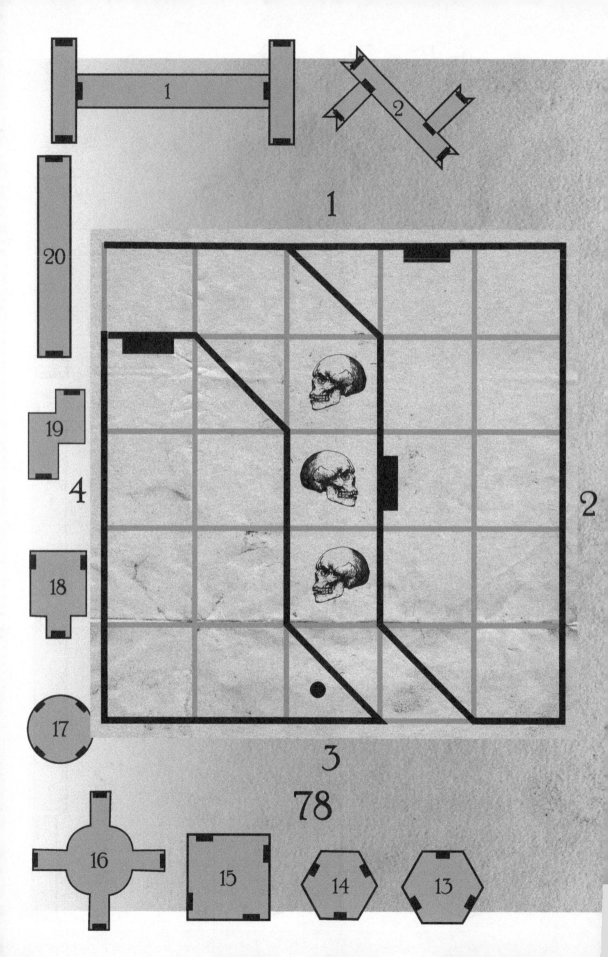

1

1

20

4

2

2

19

18

17

3

78

16

15

14

13

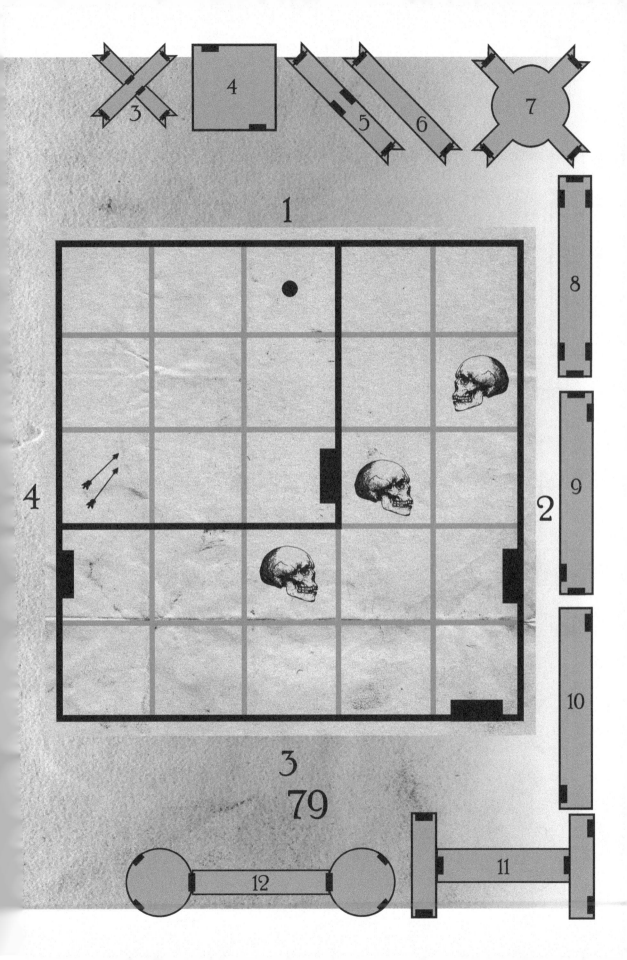

79

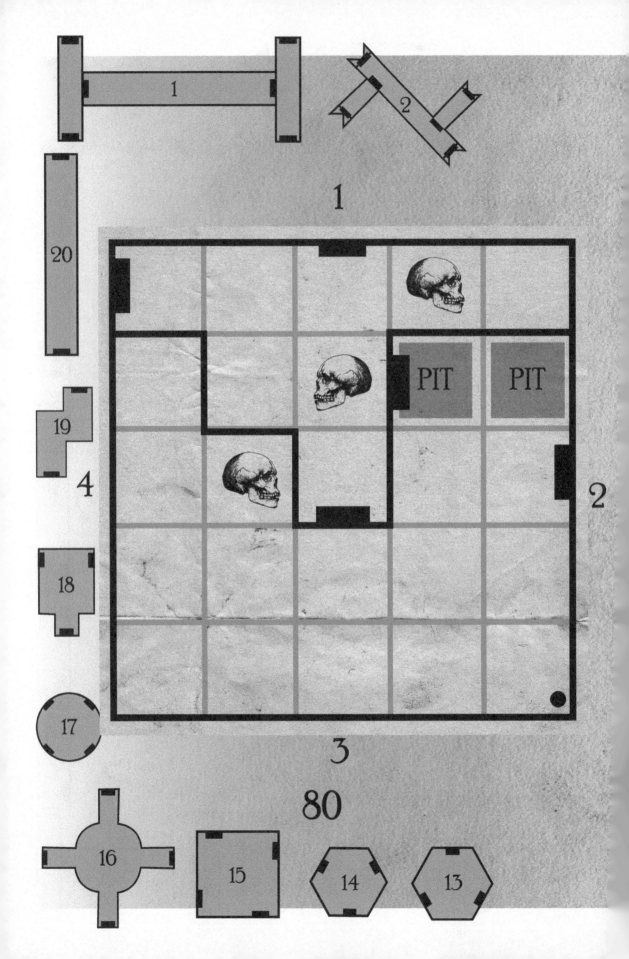

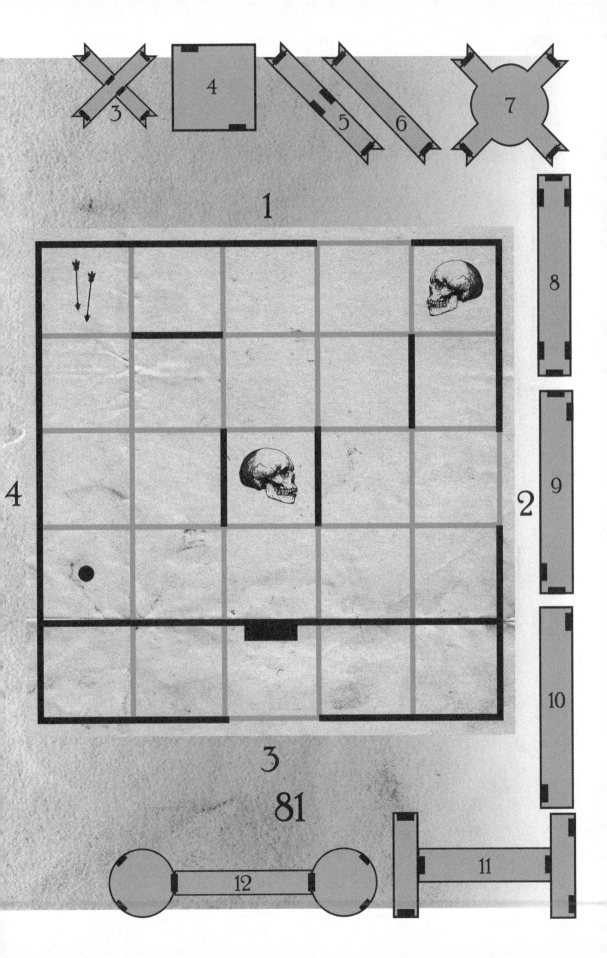

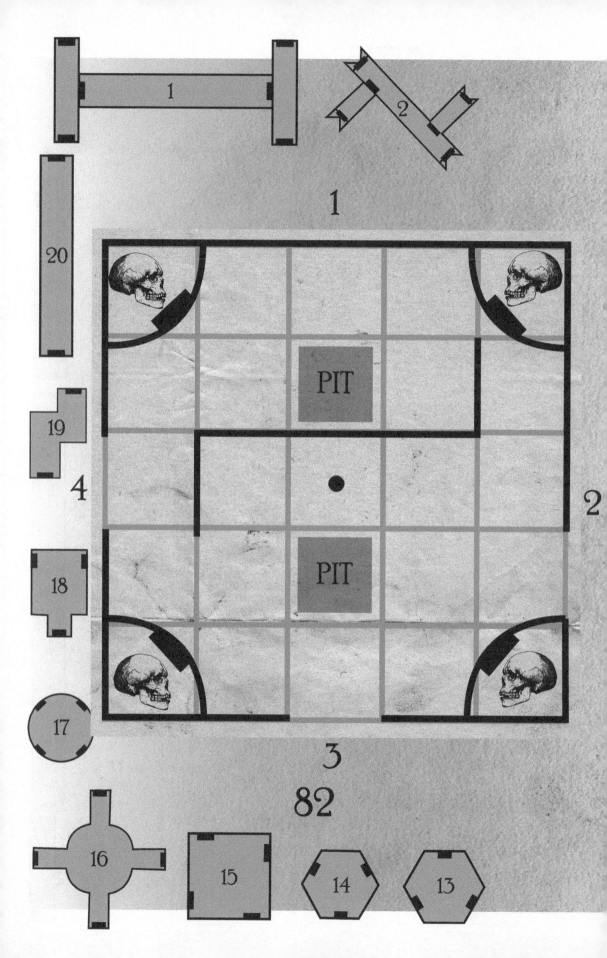

82

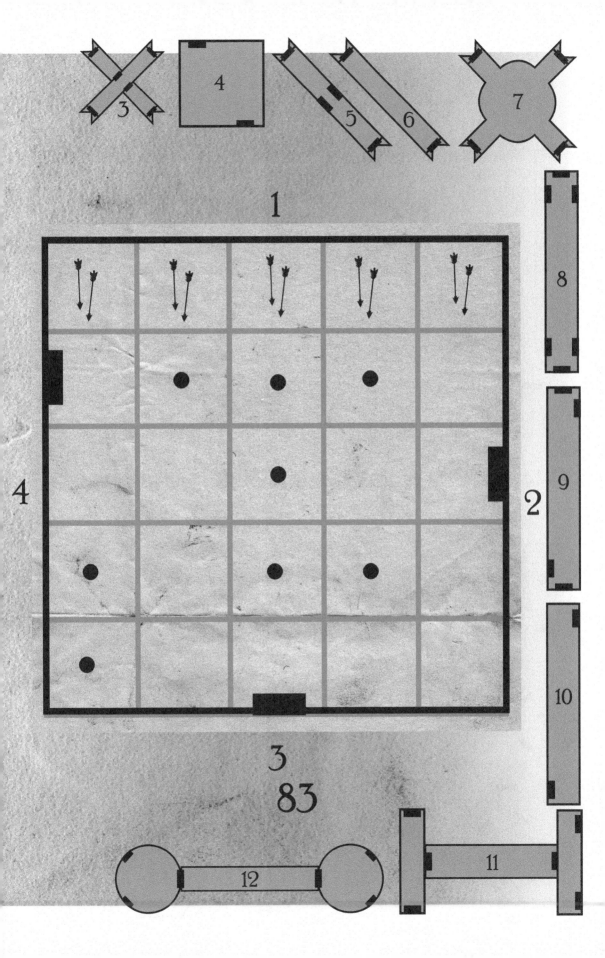

1

4

2

3

83

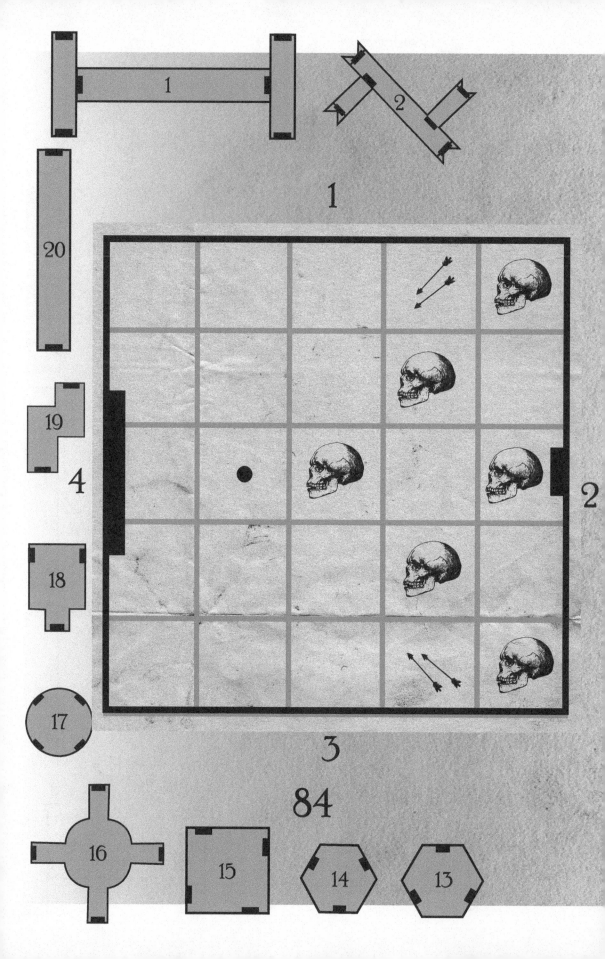

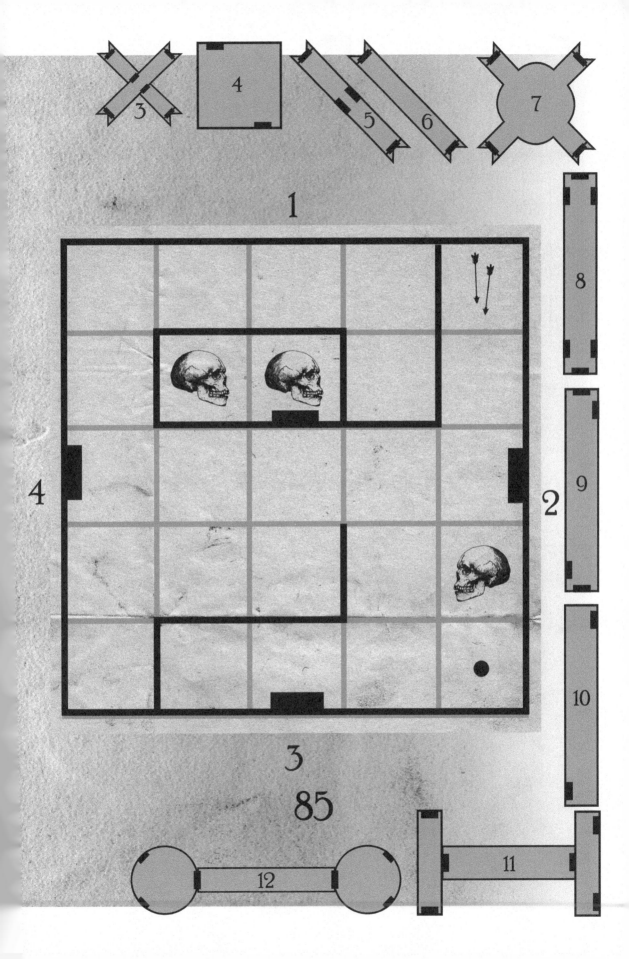

85

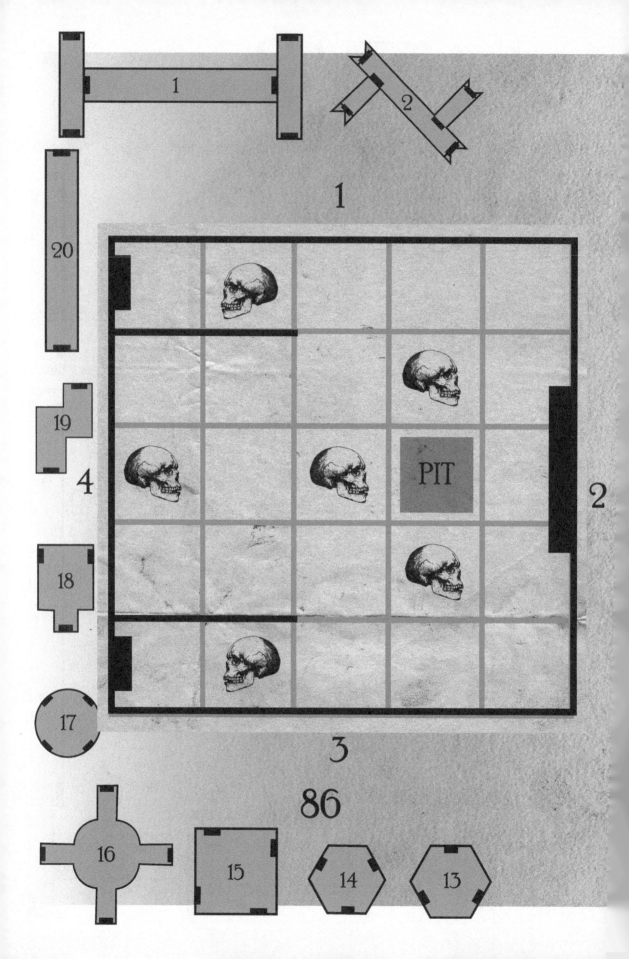

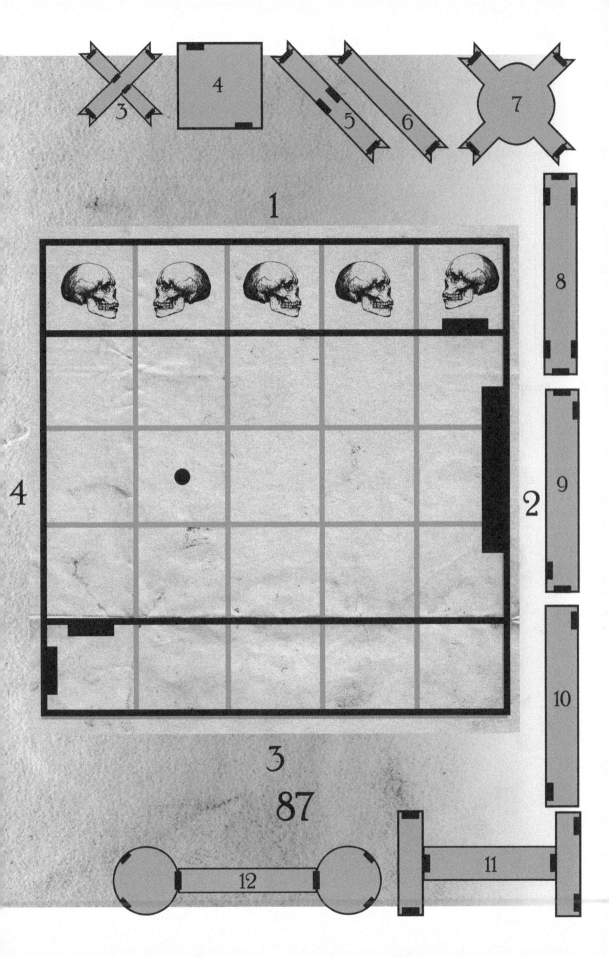

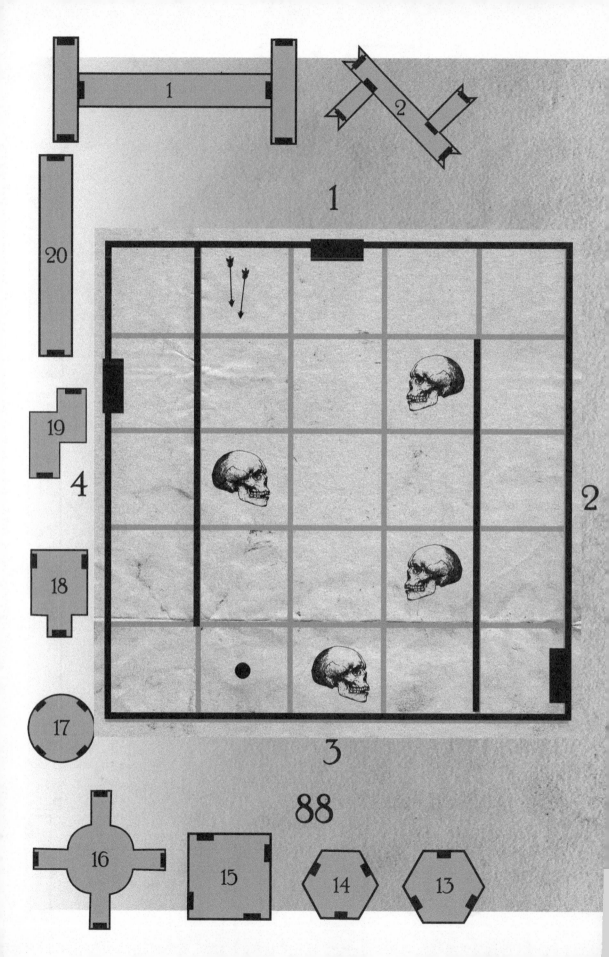

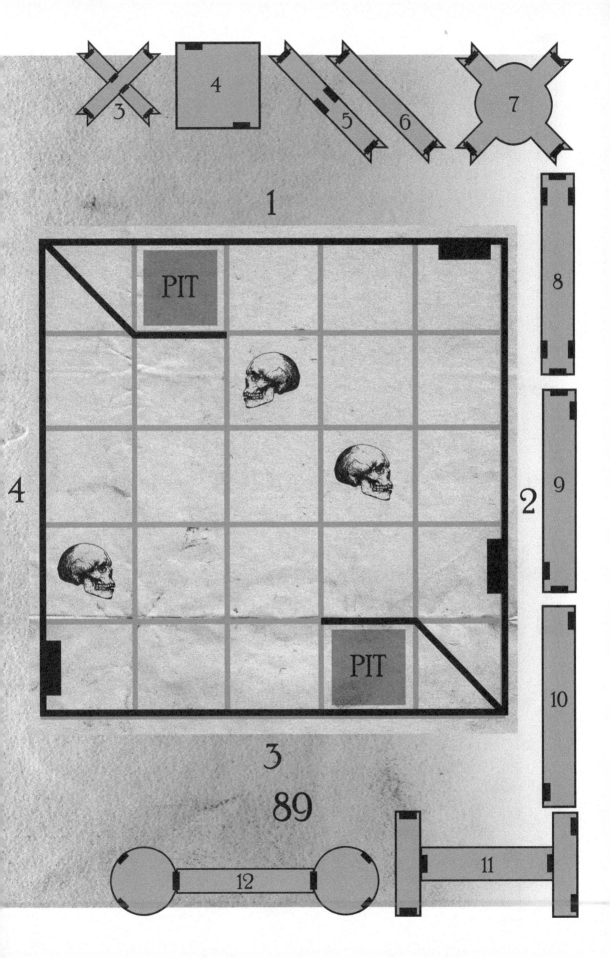

89

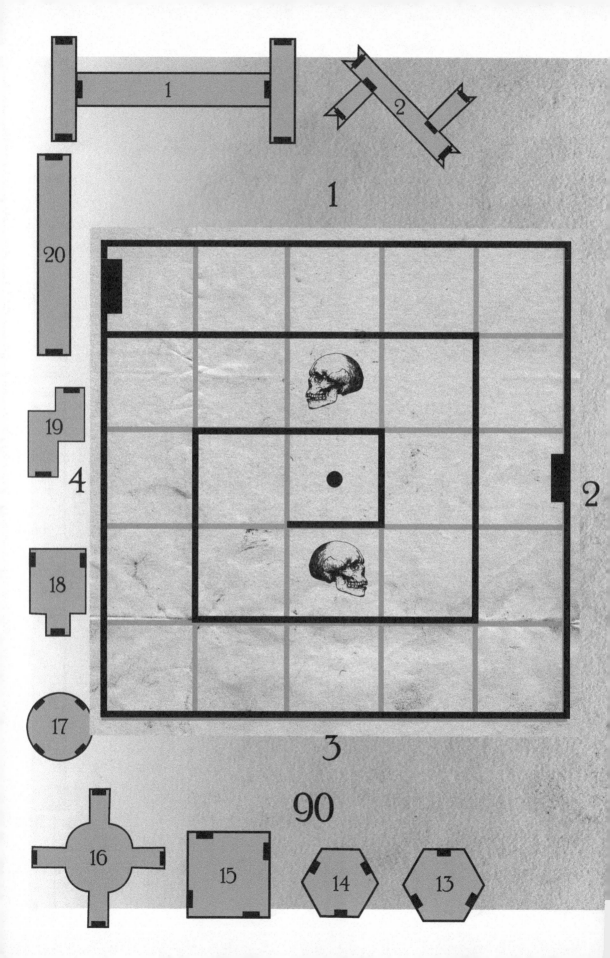

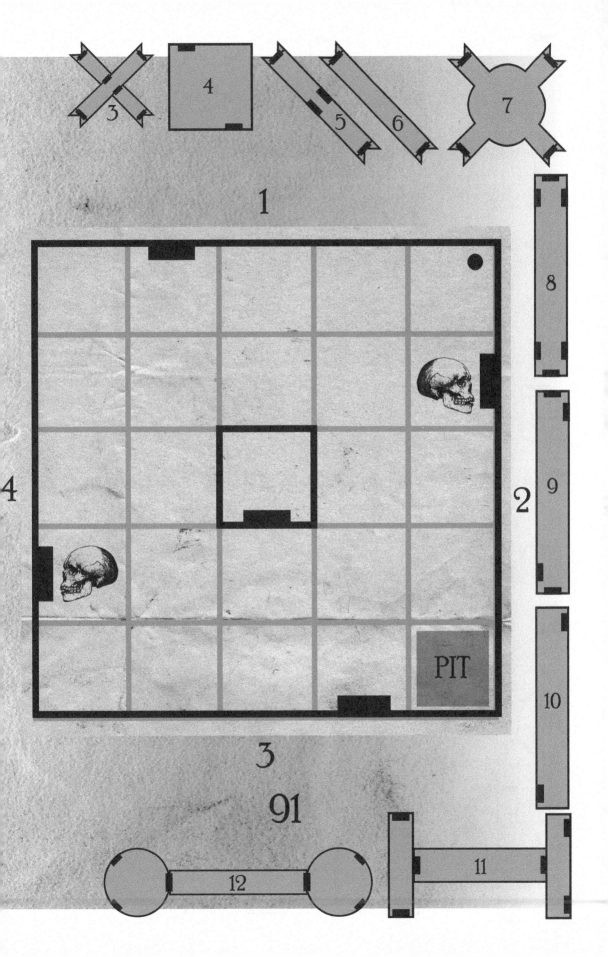

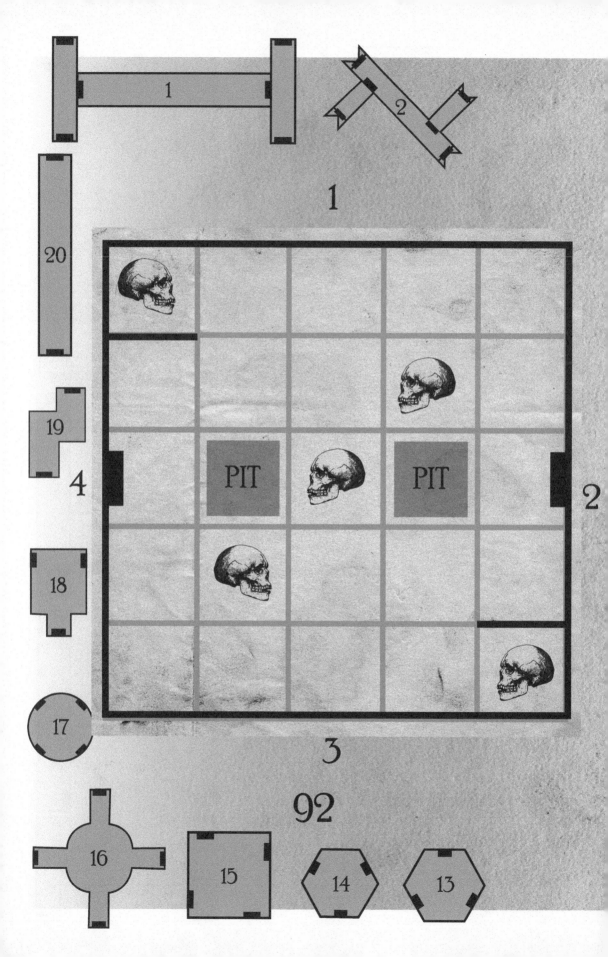

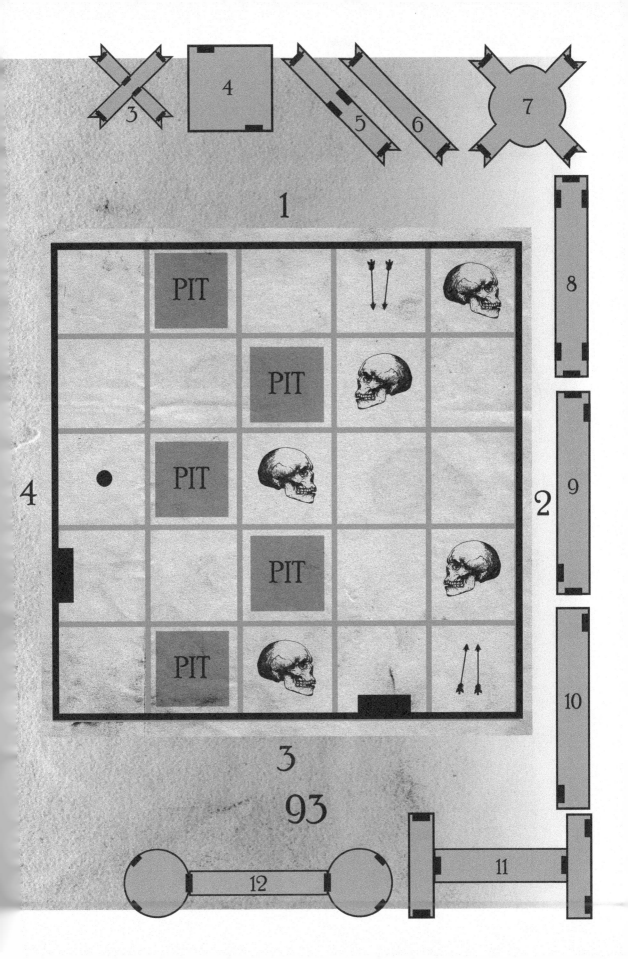

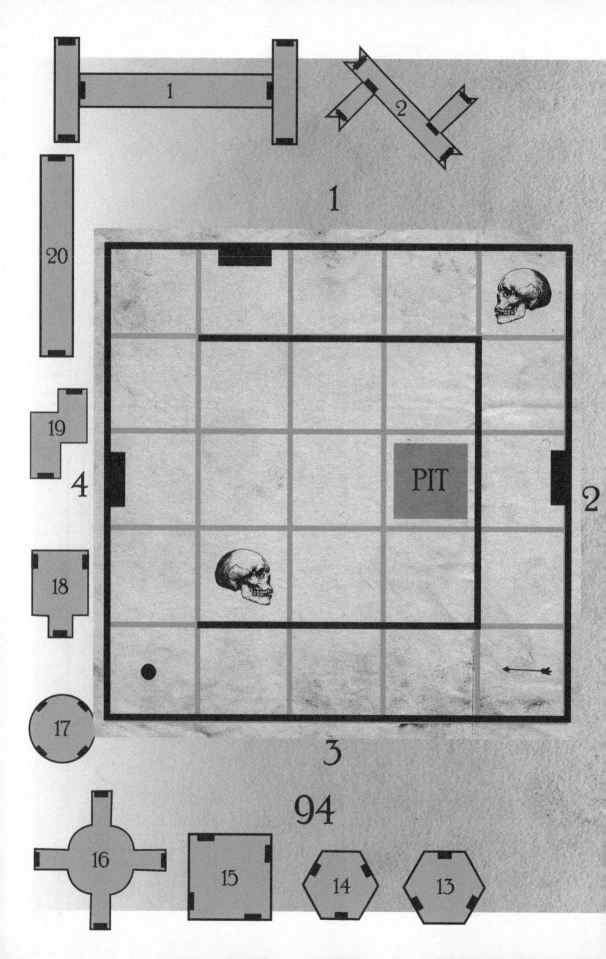

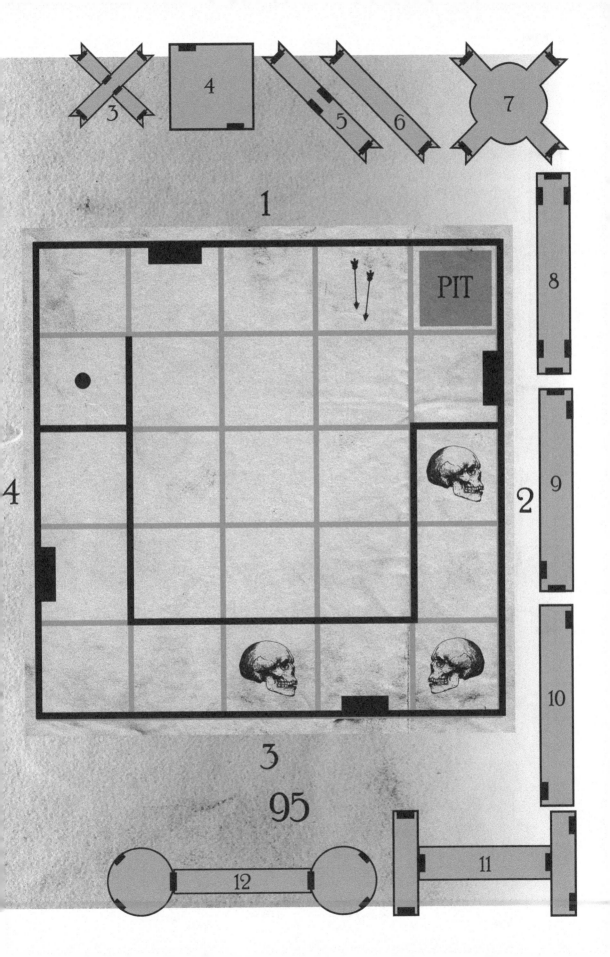

1

3

4

5

6

7

PIT

4

2

8

9

10

3

95

11

12

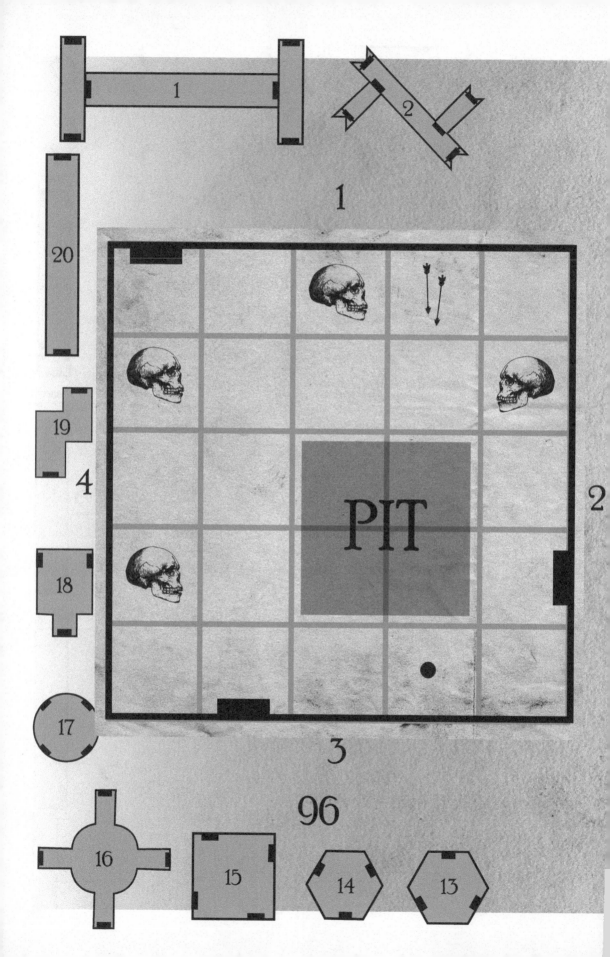

1

1

20

4

19

18

17

2

PIT

3

96

16

15

14

13

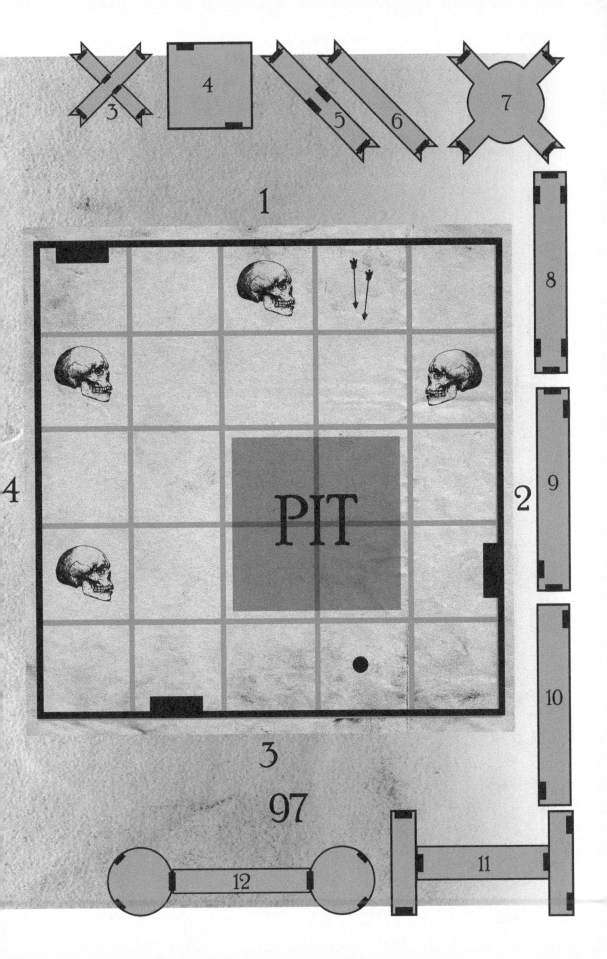

97

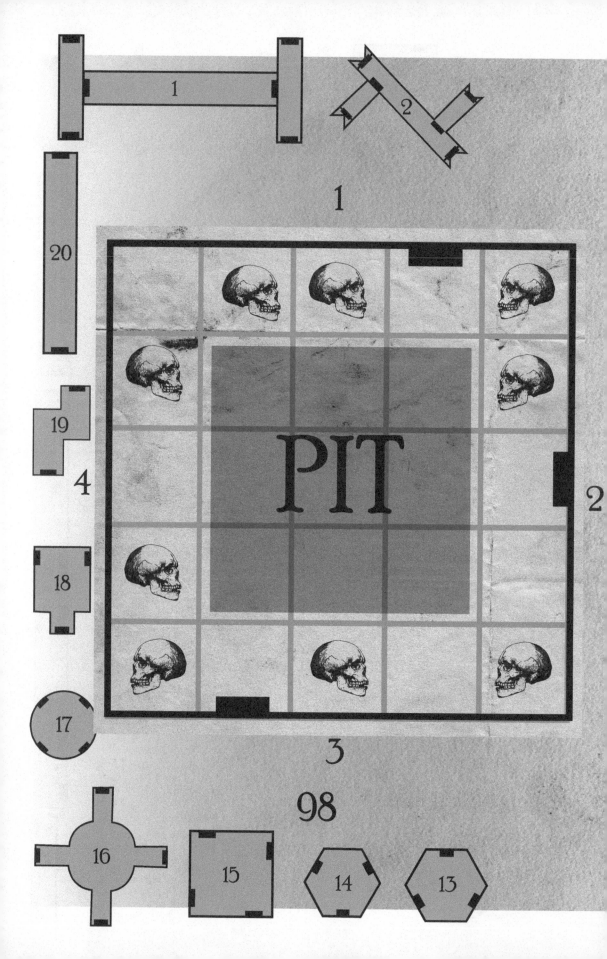

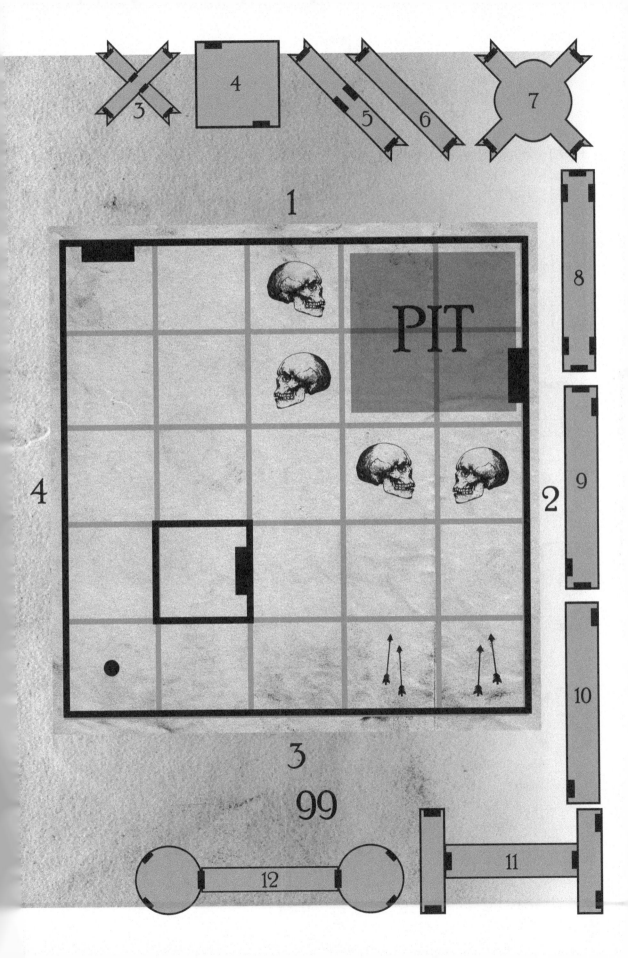

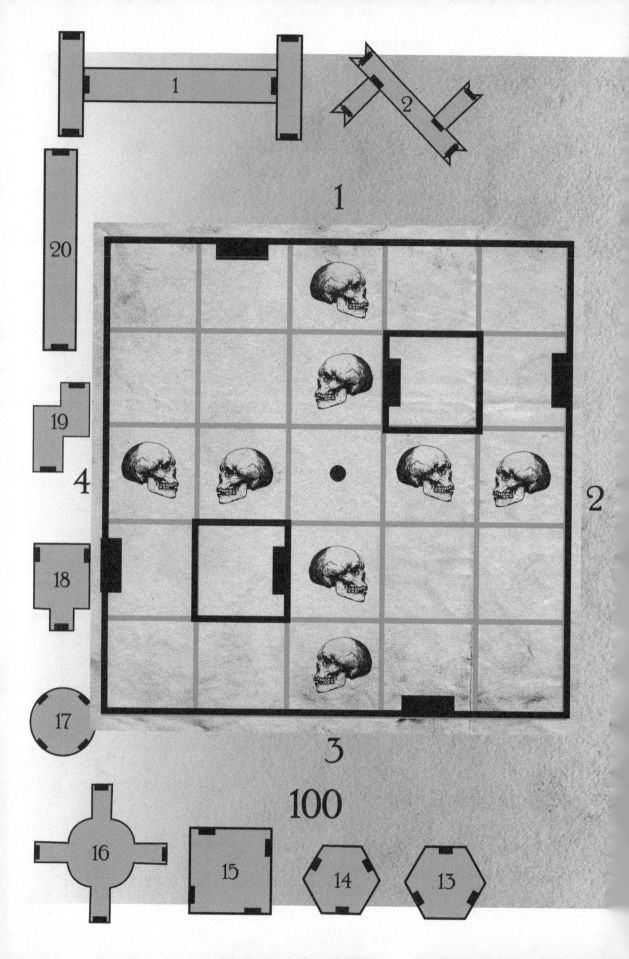

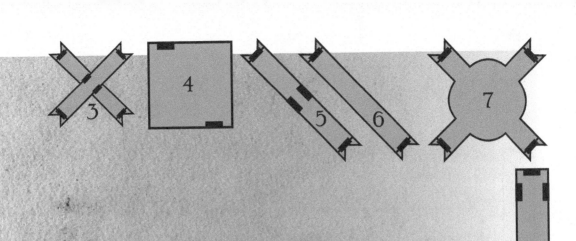

D20 BOSS
CHAMBERS

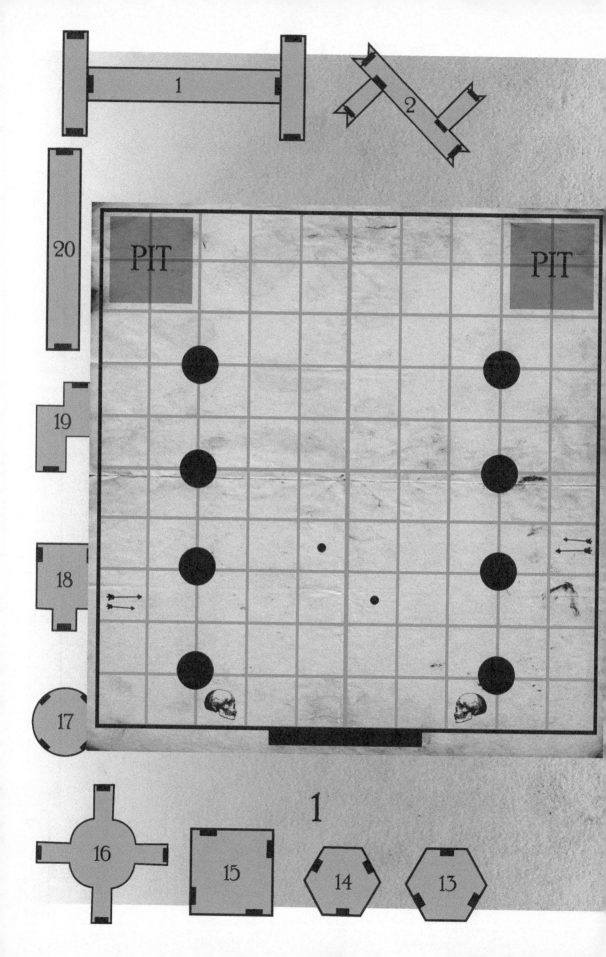

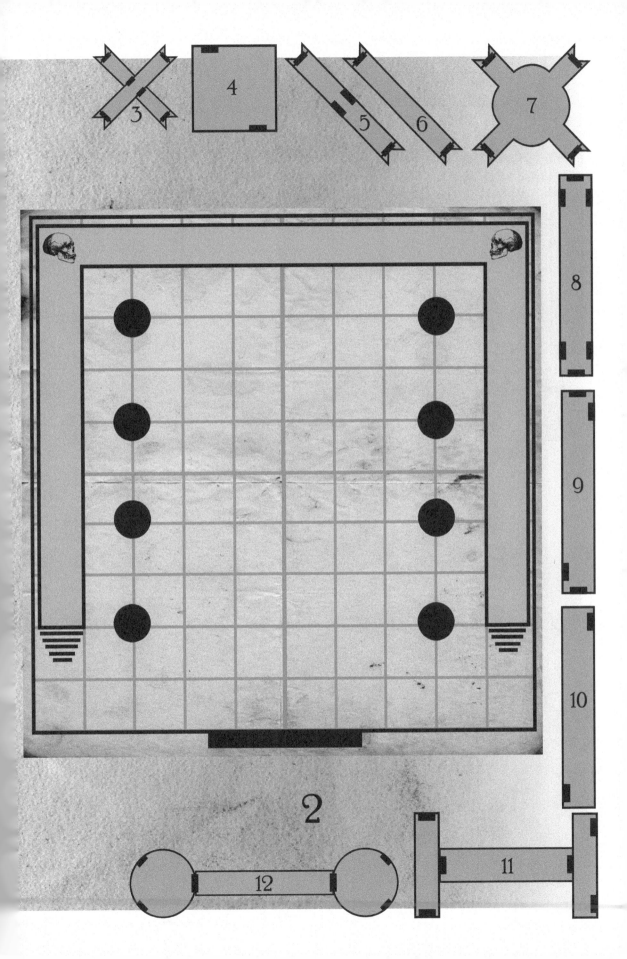

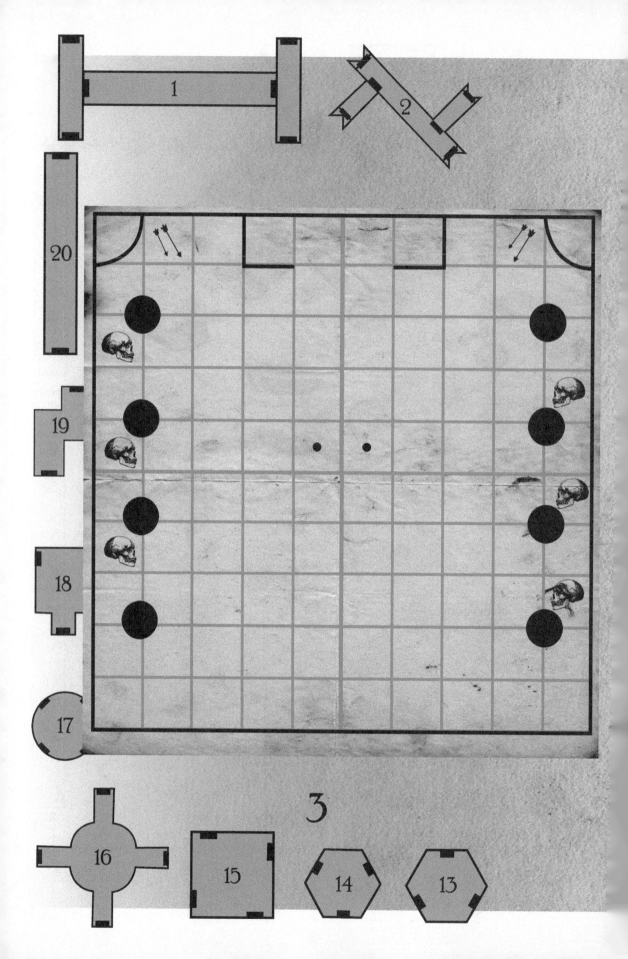

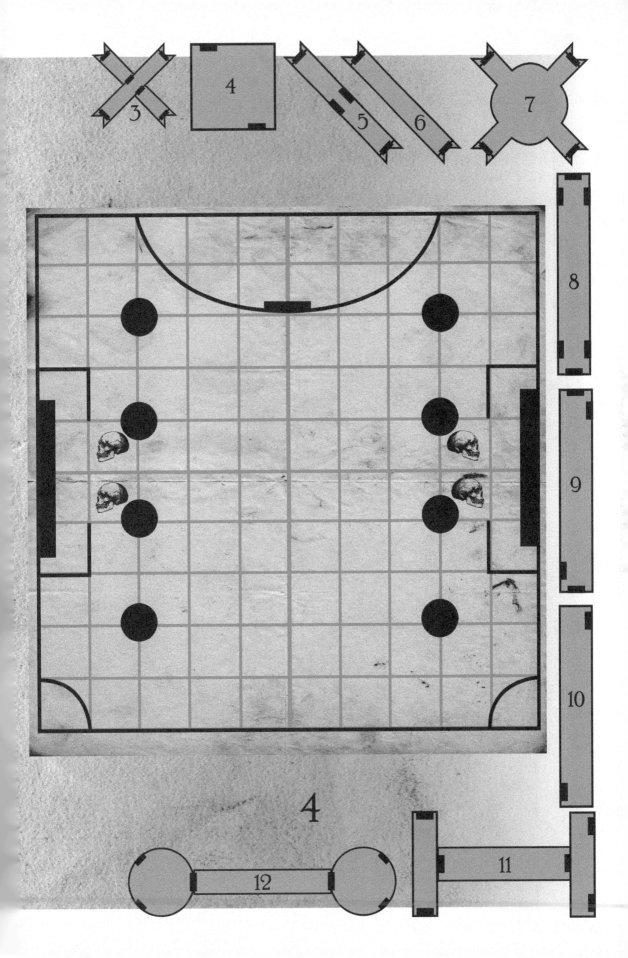

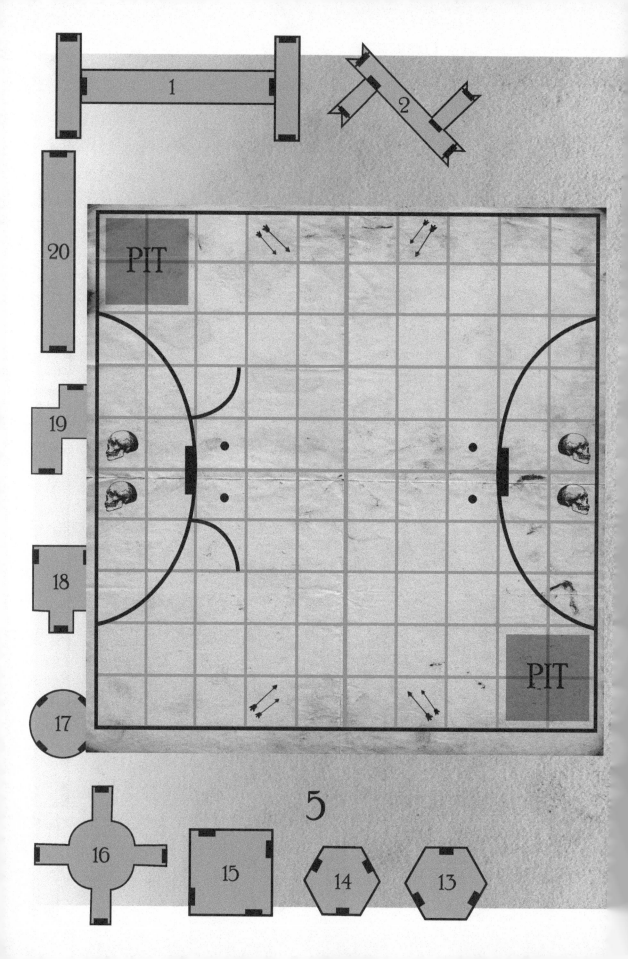

PIT

PIT

1

2

5

20

19

18

17

16

15

14

13

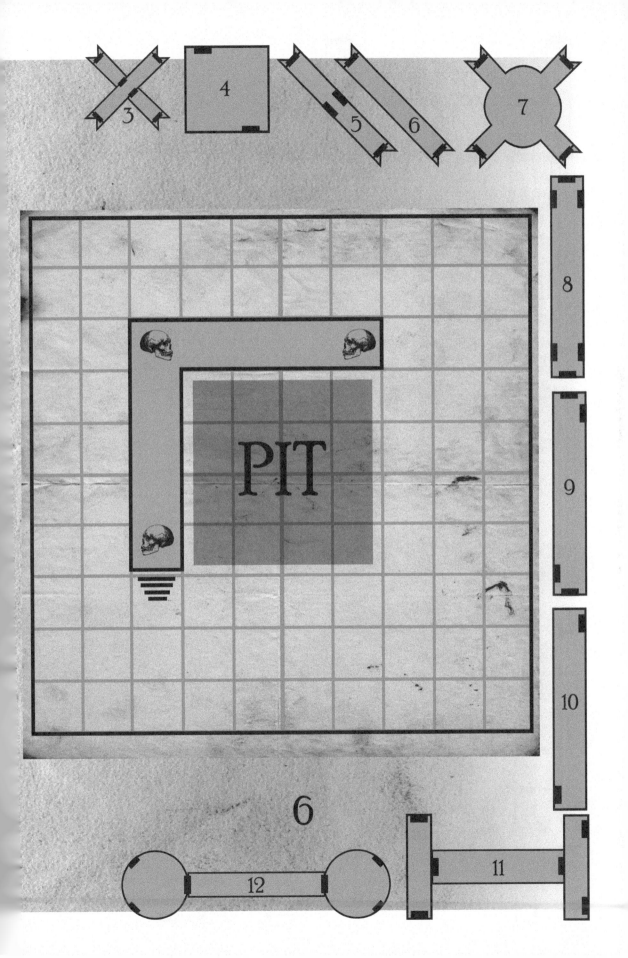

3

4

5

6

7

8

9

10

PIT

6

11

12

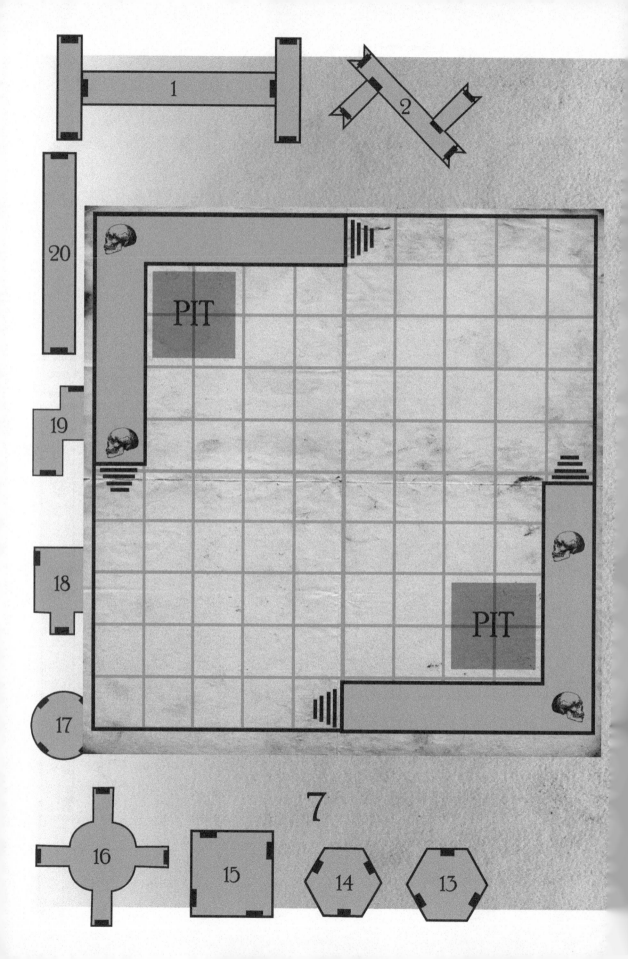

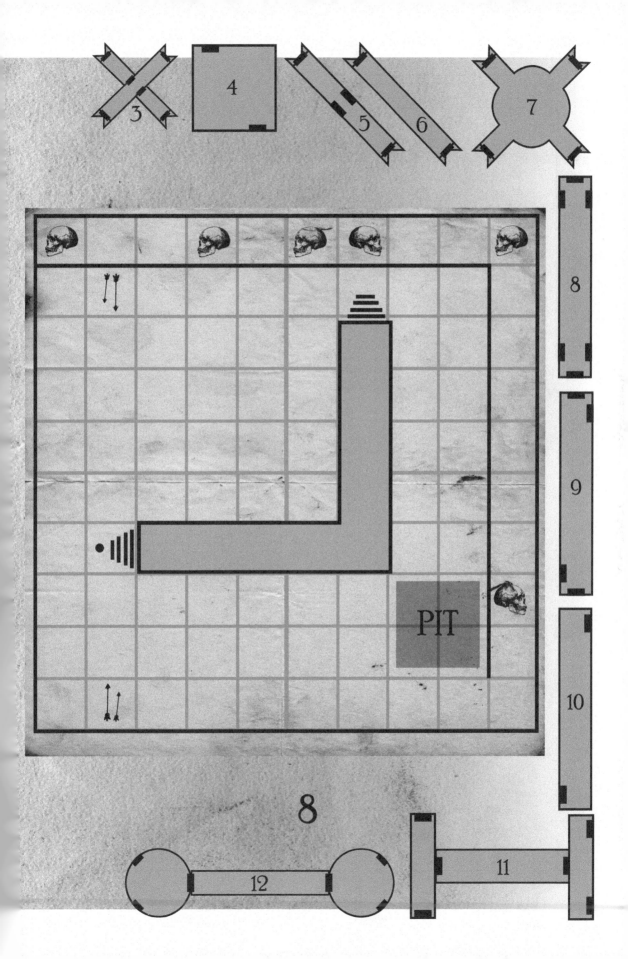

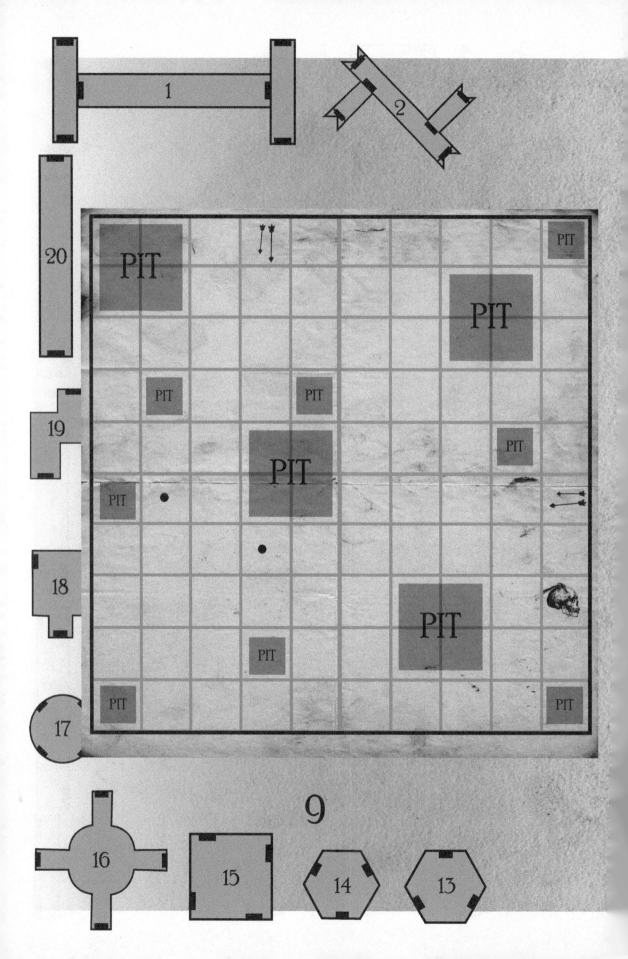

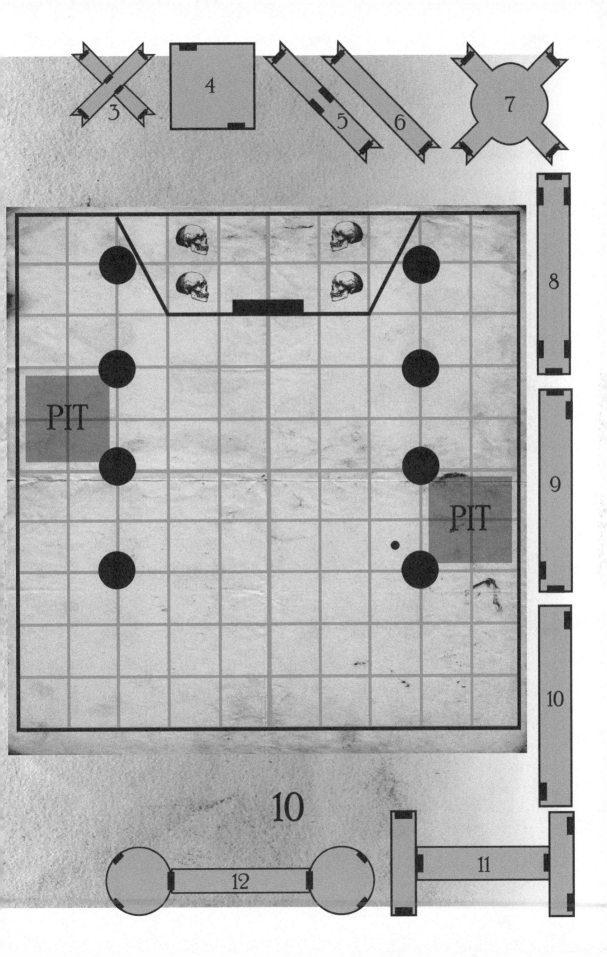

3

4

5

6

7

8

PIT

9

PIT

10

10

11

12

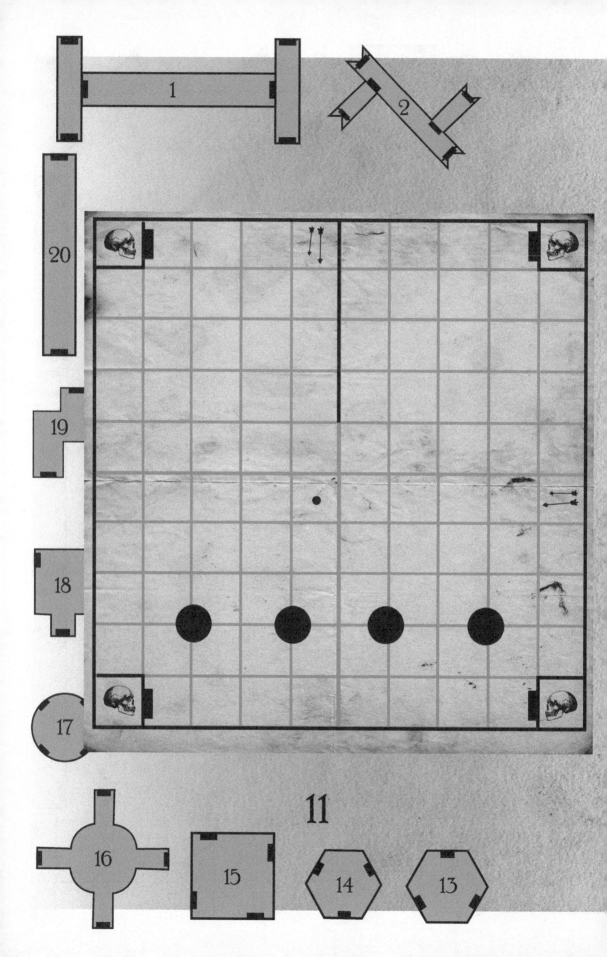

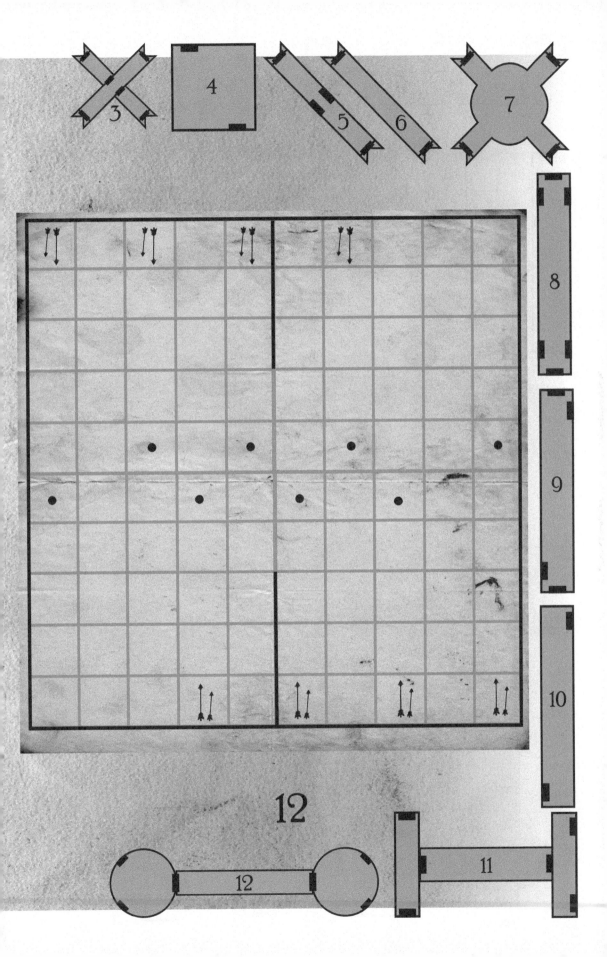

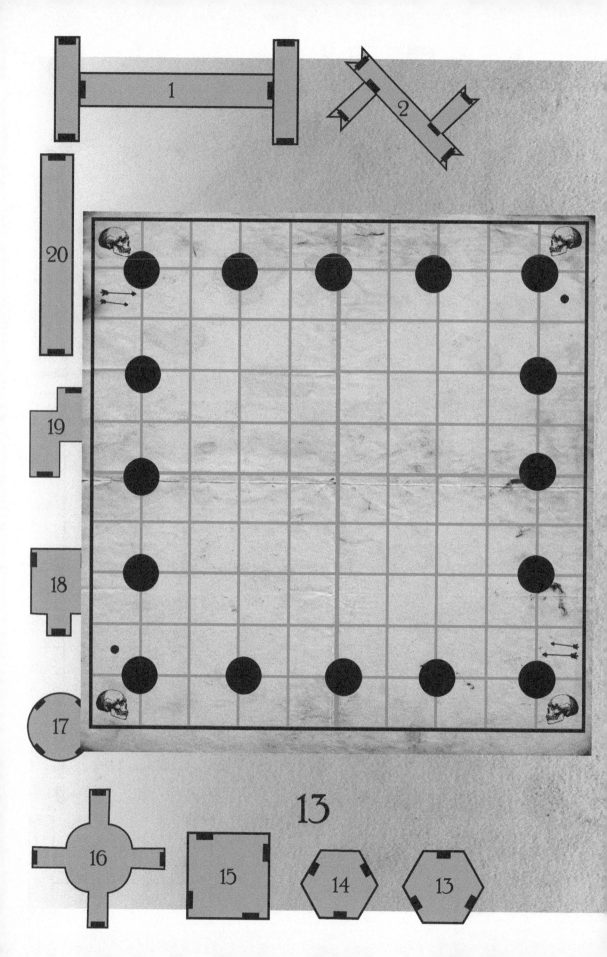

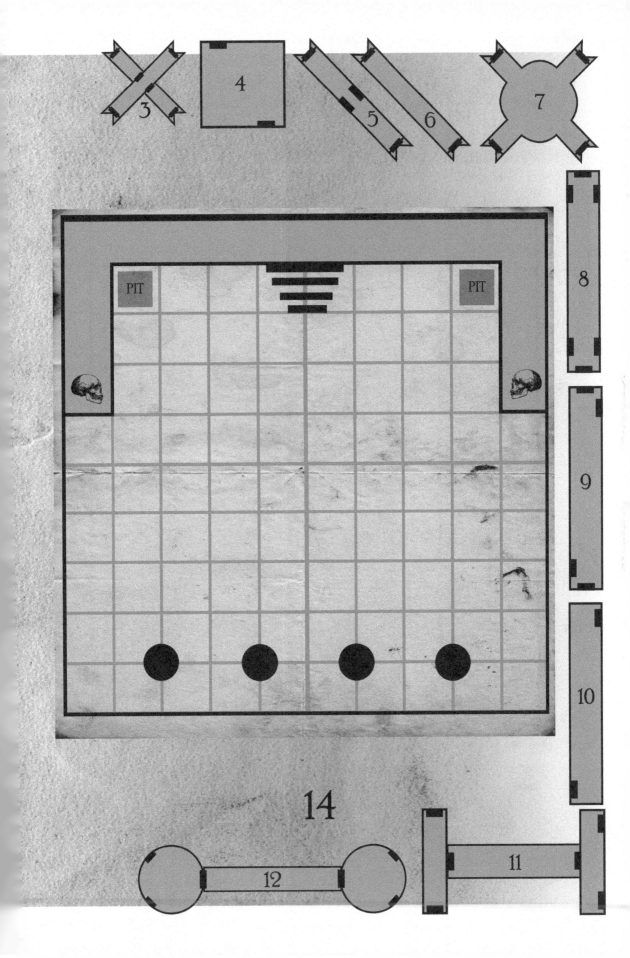

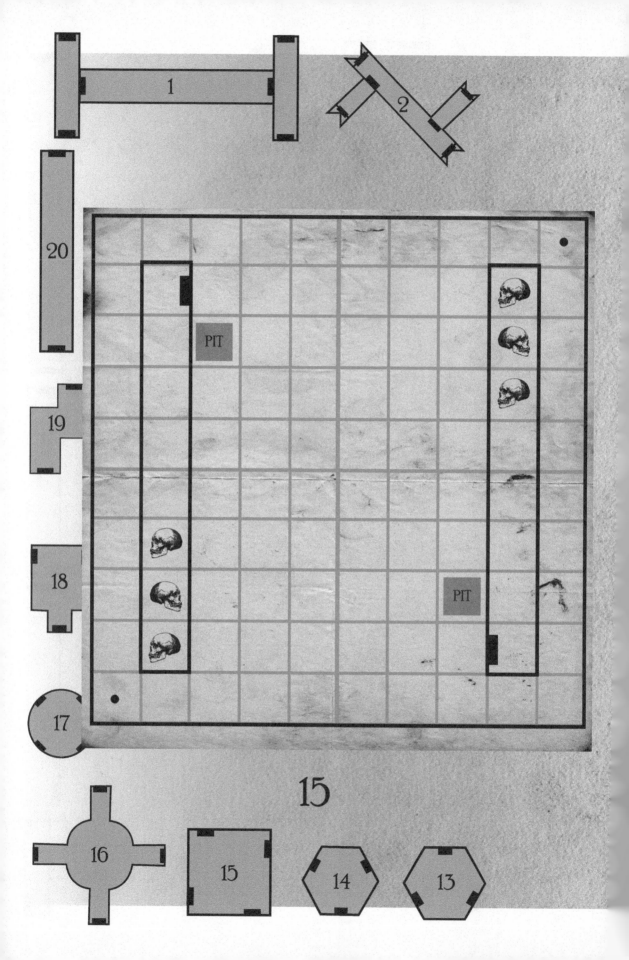

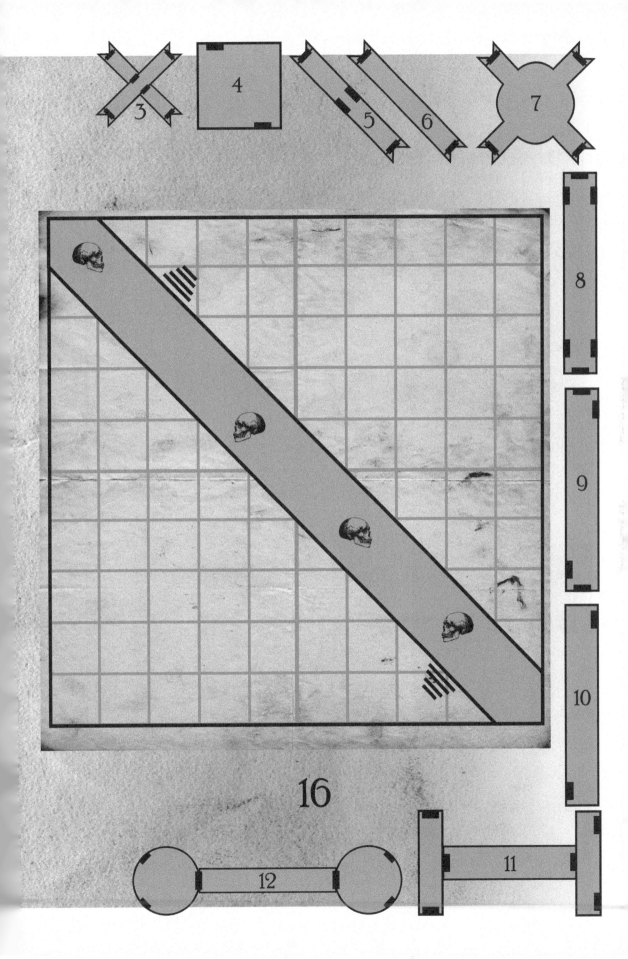

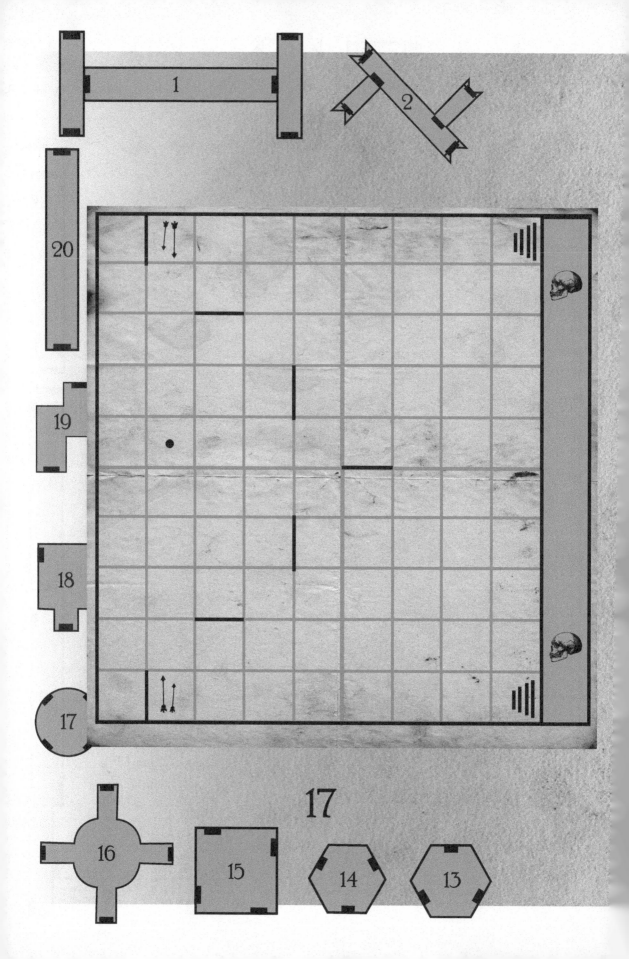

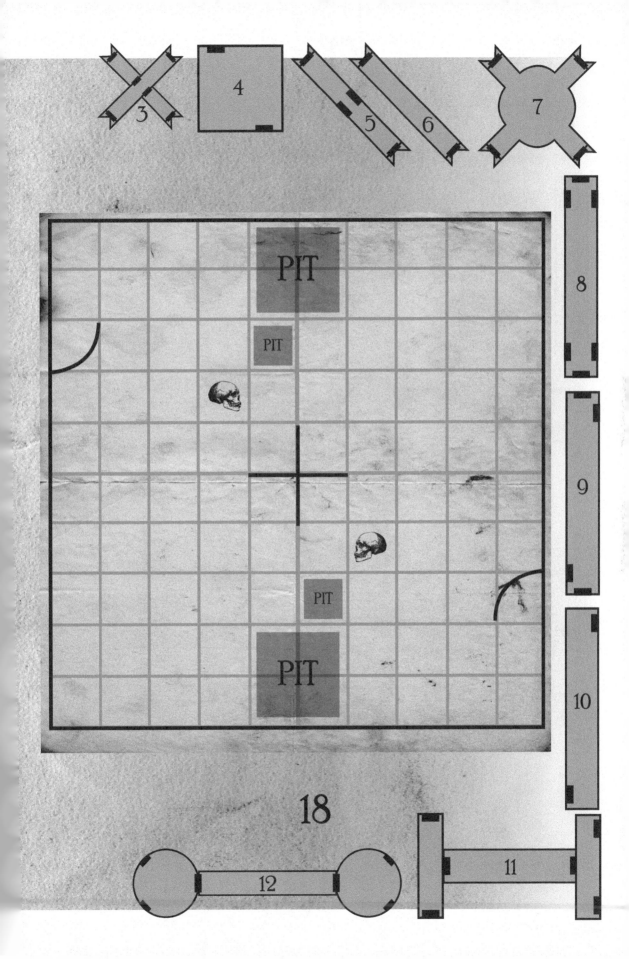

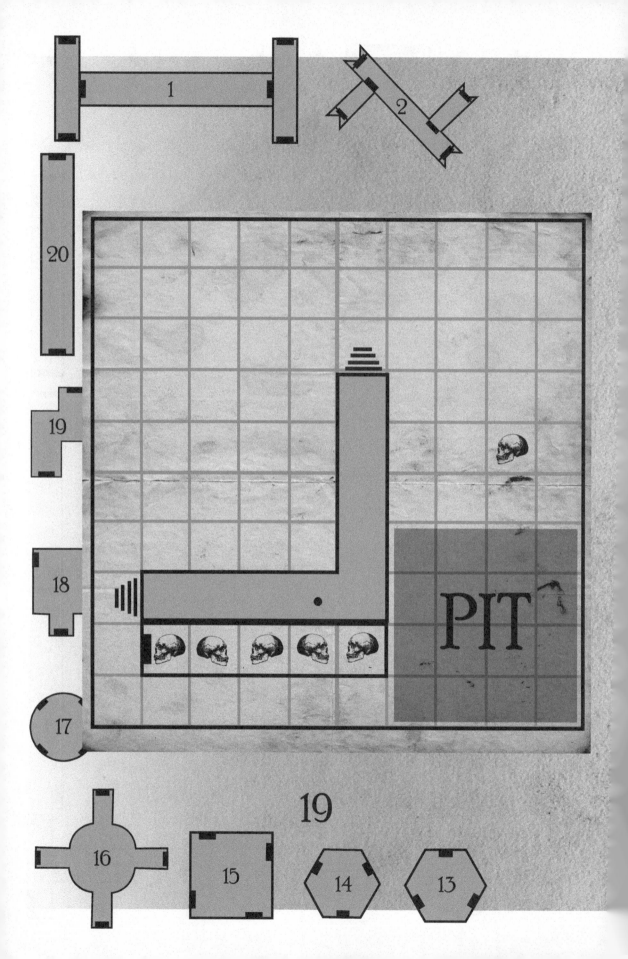

19

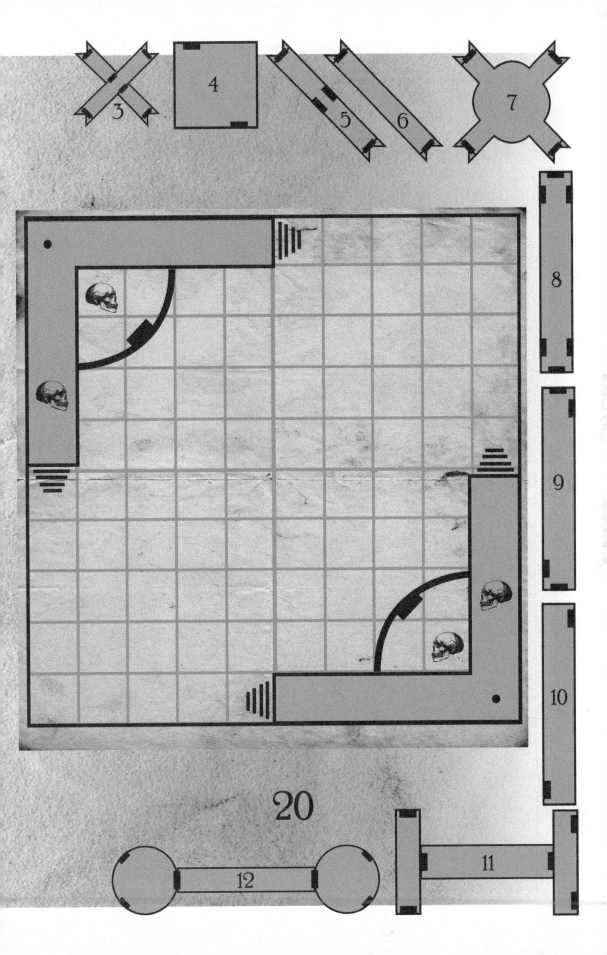

NOTES